I0580317

Love Knows No Boundaries

A Fantasy

Harvey L. Brown

Love Knows No Boundaries

Copyright © 2023 by Harvey L. Brown

All Rights Reserved

No part of this book may be reproduced or transmitted in
any form or by any means, electronic or mechanical,
including photocopying, recording, or by any information
storage and retrieval system without the written permission of
the author, except where permitted by law.

For **Ruth Letowsky,**

whose smile captivated me completely.

Acknowledgements

My deep thanks to Fran Segal, Jill and Paul Paris, and all members of Ruth's family, for their kindness in receiving me so graciously and providing an added dimension to Ruth's story.

And to these wonderful people whose advice kept me moving in the right direction: Judy Brown, Barbara Delman, Deb Doran, Pamela Grant, Jones Family, Maria Nuñez, Tiffany Pascal, Richard Rehl, Sheila Smith, Carrie Sisto, and Selwyn Woodworth.

Photo Editor: Jessica Levant

Table of Contents

Preface

First and foremost, this is a work of fiction. It does parallel my life, and I impose a documentary style on the narrative. But it remains a fantasy composed of the people, places and events in my past. All names have been changed to protect both the innocent and the guilty. All situations have been sculpted into a miscellany of what-might-have-been. If you feel the urge to smile at times, don't hold back.

With great personal satisfaction, I found that the story almost wrote itself. If my joy in writing it reflects itself in the narrative, then I have succeeded. I hope you do see it as interesting and more than a bit different.

Many novels bring with them an ethnic point of view. It can be from any people in any land. My story adopts a look at the world through the eyes of a young Jewish woman who just tried to do her job in the South in the late1960s and during the 1970s, told by the man who loved her and lost her. We follow him in his quest to win her back.

A side note: during the beginning stage of the Covid-19 outbreak in March, 2020, when science still could not help, I experienced a very scary three-plus weeks of truly devastating sickness. My survival at the time was based partly on my complete isolation, the medications I normally take, and my determination to compose the story you are about to read. Dear Ruth, in addition to the other ways you have made my life better, I think you actually helped to save my life once.

Harvey Brown May, 2021

Prologue: August, 2019

This is a story of true love that takes place though it appears that it never will happen. A story that ultimately brings two souls together even when that seems impossible. And a story that defies logic because that is the only way it makes sense.

Even today, when Boaz looked back on the events that colored his life, he still could not believe how he reacted to what transpired. Everything truly began small. It fed on his mistakes, but not entirely. There are occasions that we all set in motion, circumstances that expand beyond our control. By the time that we begin to understand what we have done, what others have manipulated in spite of us, we realize that control has slipped through our fingers, and we are undone. Welcome to the mixed-up world Boaz created for himself.

Boaz Gluzzman had no trouble making friends, especially in his earlier years. In public relations, it comes with the territory a promotion manager calls his or her own. The gist of this tale at its outset is that Boaz typically enjoyed the companionship of women without ever being more than casual about any of them.

Which brings us to the love story that began conventionally enough, until a younger version of Boaz amplified a bad situation into one that ruined what could have been a wonderful chance for happiness. Boaz lacked any preparation for the love story you are about to read. He did not deal well with it, because it took him to a new point in his life that he could not understand completely. Boaz was old enough to know how to address the situation; at the time, he was just not as experienced with women as he thought he was. Poor Boaz.

As Boaz himself will tell you, "I find that I get better with age at seeking and staying on the road to the correct answer. But it took me a lifetime to figure that out."

His tale begins exactly fifty years after it ended. Now, stay with the storyline; you will figure things out long before the youthful Mr. Gluzzman did. The time is August, 2019. Boaz made a discovery that flooded his head with the pieces of a long-forgotten story. In the beginning, as he sought to put together the remnants of those details, Boaz remembered mentioning to his friend Rocky - you will meet him later - that in August of 1969, he fell in love with a marvelous woman. Rocky pointed out that during that month exactly fifty years earlier, Charles Manson and his clique of women murdered and were convicted for killing actress Sharon Tate. Rocky added that during that same month, a concert took place near Bethel, NY called Woodstock. He said he looked forward to the full version of my story as my contribution to that very newsworthy month. A person needs friends like Rocky. He has a perspective that never loses sight of reality.

When Boaz made his coffee each morning, he adhered to his system. Everything he did had a precise order. He never varied from it. Essentially, he did not even have to think about getting his coffee brewed. His brain, comfortable with the repetition, performed seemingly without his participation.

But one morning, the coffee pot broke. It would not turn on. He simply stared at it as his mind grappled with what happened. Betrayed by the appliance, Boaz ran to the local coffee shop to fulfill his morning ritual.

Satisfied for the moment, he had to decide what to do with that expensive coffee pot. He called a friend who thought it could be repaired. Boaz decided to put the appliance aside until he had time to take it in to the repair shop. He looked around. All the usual places to store things were full at the moment.

There, in the corner of a shelf, he saw the answer. If he could just move that old, small filing cabinet, he would have room for the coffee pot. So with more ambition than strength, Boaz lifted the five-drawer cabinet. It was unexpectedly heavy, prompting him to put it down and open the drawers one by one.

What on Earth made this easy task so difficult? Boaz found out, and it changed his life.

"I hate moving furniture," Boaz stated with a certainty that left no doubt as to its truthfulness. "Not only does it resemble work, it upsets the order of things," he added. That small, metal filing cabinet, roughly eleven by eleven inches and slightly deeper, had been sitting on the shelf for years . . . no, decades.

The five tiny drawers could each hold no more than a medium-sized manilla folder or two. Once a year Boaz would deposit in one drawer the copies of those annual tax returns we all enjoy complaining about. That was all he used the filing cabinet for.

Boaz had long ago forgotten what the other drawers contained, and so, never opened them. Unlike Alice, he never ventured down the rabbit hole to investigate the contents of the other drawers.

Then, Boaz needed the space for something else. Grudgingly, he lifted a very heavy, though small, filing cabinet. His Federal and State tax copies should not have weighed so much were the actual incomes factored in. Evidence from his earlier days in public relations provided much of the weight responsible for his complaint. Old letterhead from places he would never live again, brochures that deserved a quick trip to the wastebasket, and one file contributed to this weighty mess. Boaz dispatched them all, except the tax forms and the file.

He simply could not throw out proof that he once made $11.11 per week at an after- school job some three years before he entered the university. Such humble beginnings should be remembered, no matter how minuscule they seem today. The file, on the other hand, was a different matter. It was labeled only with his name: Boaz Gluzzman. He remembered vaguely what it contained: press releases and references to himself in various local newspaper columns mentioning and detailing his somewhat meteoric rise through the world of public relations, at least if you listen to Boaz' version of his slightly exaggerated story. In those long-ago days, every mention of his name in print resounded with him. The file chronicled his complete work history, right up until the television job in Buffalo, NY. Then it stopped.

Fascinated, Boaz sought more information on this character who took shape as he read about him.

"It was me, and I read about me as one completely divorced from the person I already knew. 'Born and educated in Philadelphia, he left the University of Pennsylvania in the late 1950s to conquer the public relations world. He worked in Philly, later in New York City and Buffalo'," concluded Boaz.

Young people, he decided, enjoy scampering around the country in search of ever-changing horizons. The youth and energy of that person he was once had disappeared, gone with the mist and clouded by years of experiences and vanishing hopes.

He turned the page, deciding he was finished with reading about himself in the third person. Behind the news

The metal cabinet

items and press releases that reminded Boaz of his early working years, a few 8"x10" photographs with dates came into view. If he could have realized then that looking at these photos would change his life, he might have hesitated. But no, he did not pause.

Upon reflection, Boaz was glad he saw those photos from fifty years ago. He looked at the photo of a woman he met in August, 1969. Exactly half a century earlier — to the month! How strange is that? And the strangest thing of all, though he did not realize it at the time, was that it had already changed his life.

Three different pictures of a beautiful woman he had met in Hollywood occupied his thoughts. As Boaz looked and remembered, it began to take possession of his brain. Details began to flood over him. Not all at once. Slowly, over the hours and days that followed. He knew right away who she was. But it became apparent that he had blocked her memory, and he was going to need help to restore her to her place in his life after fifty years. Boaz knew her name, Judith. He knew that she, like him, held the position of promotion manager. And slowly, he began to remember some of the details of their brief relationship. They were young. She was five years younger than his thirty- three years. They were both Jewish, and their attachment, though brief, was genuine. His brain grasped at other details that lay just outside his reach.

The Internet held the answer. It always amazed him how much you can learn about someone simply by entering their name. He willingly admitted that his motivation turned to obsession for a short while, and he joined two, maybe three, search engines as he sought to put flesh on this woman who absolutely commanded his full attention throughout the entire week.

He learned that she had an older sister and a large family of relatives who adored her, including a niece and nephew named Esty and Max, whom she chose to live with in Atlanta for a short while until she died in 2013. Having lived on her own for all her adult life, only a drastic setback could have altered her lifestyle. The search engines could no longer help Boaz. He called the chapel where her burial service took place, and they told him where she was buried.

Boaz was devastated. He had neglected her for fifty years, and she had not waited for him. He wished out loud that he could bring her back to life. How presumptuous of him. No one chooses to die, at least not in the normal course of events.

Someday, he would discover what had happened to her. Today was not that day. Perhaps soon. While dying in your seventies is not uncommon, he felt some illness or disease had brought it on. Boaz had to know and decided that he would find out.

Moreover, she never married, and he had no idea why. That question alone disturbed him most of all. Was a new phase of his life just beginning?

Some people would choose this moment to close that chapter of their lives. Boaz could not shrug off Judith's death, even though it happened so long ago. If anything, it provided questions that he felt needed to be answered. Why did he feel this way?

That portion of his life had passed. As he shaved that morning, Boaz settled on the one word that could explain the way he felt: guilt. He had not abused her. Far from it, he had met her and would go as far as to say he loved her. But he could not even say that, because her memory was still creeping back into his thoughts. Was he responsible for why she died? Probably not. Was he the reason she never married? Boaz could not bring himself to answer that question. He simply could not face finding out that answer.

He looked in the mirror. Looking back at him was the man who could be suspected of messing up his whole life by not pursuing this woman to at least find out if he should have gotten to know her and perhaps marry her.

Let this be a lesson for all who have trouble making up their mind: life turns on our smallest, seemingly inconsequential decisions. And it is unforgiving. Life cares not whether you are young or old, smart or not, in command of the situation or simply an onlooker. When you must make a decision, make it. Right or wrong, make the choice.

Chapter One

Boaz Meets Judith:
Hollywood, 1969

Boaz Gluzzman was the promotion manager for the United Broadcasting Network outlet in Buffalo. The story that changed his life happened across the country in Tinseltown. No, it was not scripted by a Hollywood writer. At best, it could have been the product of a movie with music. But it was not.

Judith and Boaz met at a national promotion group session staged in Hollywood. Ah, Hollywood. He never went there to be in the movies, not even to go to the movies.

Many of us rhapsodize about that city-within-a-city. Hollywood churns out movie upon movie extolling its own virtues, of which it has few. Nevertheless, it has been an effective magnet for the young and the inspired, for the penniless and the privileged.

Much of the evening entertainment that appeared on UBN came to life in the Hollywood picture studios. All the major television networks used Tinseltown as the major source of their evening programs. UBN was no different. So in the late summer, when the sun shone brightly and the young kids had finally put school out of their minds, TV networks began their push for viewership domination in the fall.

They had to stay ahead of public trends, and in the process, tell the public exactly what it was they wanted all along. This included the elaborate in-gathering of representatives from each of their affiliate stations throughout the United States. The promotion managers who sold their respective networks to the public needed strong incentive. So the networks gathered them at the source to show them how well Hollywood knows how to put on a show.

In August, 1969, Boaz went to Hollywood as one of a few hundred promotion managers in the country to preview the new, upcoming fall shows on the UBN. It was work. Nice work, with a hectic schedule. UBN made sure all the promotion managers met a few movie stars, toured the studios, dressed up for extravagant dinners, and saw promos on upcoming fall shows. It was really stressful. Actually, that was not meant to be even slightly amusing. The national network kept them jumping and moving to their tune over the course of those several days. They wanted their money's worth. What all those young and eager promotion managers wanted was a good time. To be fair, both the network and their managers got what they desired.

It was there that Boaz met a young lady named Judith Brasilov, then the promotion manager for UBN in Atlanta, GA. They knew each other for only a few days. They connected. Both of them felt something. It surprised Boaz; it surprised Judith. No bells rang; no cannons went off. Well, maybe just a small howitzer in his head. Boaz wished he could say that he realized what was going on at the time. He did not. Something was going on; that much even he could figure out. Boaz is someone who makes an honest effort to stay away from clichés. Still, he would not offer much of a counter- argument if you were to say it was love at first sight.

Now there are a couple of ways to interpret this. Many of us, Boaz included, would read the encounter as a good reason for quick, explosive and deeply satisfying physical sex. That did happen. What also occurred was a connection much more dangerous: an instantaneous suspicion that both were meeting someone with whom they would gladly spend the rest of their lives. No physical explosions, just a quiet recognition and understanding that they fit, that they were comfortable with each other, that at that moment the world had paused, and they were the reason.

If you have ever encountered a moment like that in your life, you know the feeling. It is as overwhelming as it is sudden. And you are clueless as to the meaning of what is happening. Boaz got that it amounted to something important. More than that eluded his confused brain.

People equate finding love with the swell of string music. Perhaps in the movies and on television. What he will tell you is, it comes without cue cards, without any melody, and maybe, just maybe, you can figure out there is something going on. That does not mean you are stupid or dense or completely unaware of love in the air. You realize how important the time is. At that moment, you must figuratively pick yourself up and begin to make sense of what is happening. And if you utter a few incoherent thoughts, and fumble opening a door, or forget your own name, you will figure it out. Just not at this moment.

Rarely does Boaz use the word dangerous to describe his relationship with a woman. That is because it symbolizes the strongest, most deeply-felt connection he could have with another person. It transcends any description you might use, any descriptive word ending in …e-s-t that you could formulate in your mind. So please, do not overlook that Boaz used it without prompting with Judith. In fact, he could not get the word nor the woman out of his mind during their time in Hollywood.

They went everywhere together. Mostly, UBN kept them scurrying from pilot programs of new shows to production studios to see where new or established TV shows were filmed. They kept everyone moving, and Judith and Boaz moved together.

On the last evening before they departed for home, a full-dress gala took place. For guys, this meant a nice suit and tie. For women, it became an all-out assault on beauty. Dresses in the predominant fashion of 1969 using exquisite fabrics, complemented by hair styles and makeup guaranteed to turn the head of every poor wretch they chose to shine their carefully concocted aura upon. It worked.

Boaz could only answer for himself. In the late 1960s, you were bowled over by what you saw. Fortunately, Boaz had resolved to stand his ground. He prepared himself for Judith's well-thought-out wardrobe and perfect countenance. It was not easy to be resolute. That dangerous lady looked stunning tonight. Boaz determined that as a perfect gentleman, he would say those polite remarks everyone made in such a situation. His first inane and stupid words of praise were about to come out, when she smiled. Her smile was just not fair; Boaz was unprepared for it.

That did it. He forgot all his carefully constructed rules. In front of far too many people, he grabbed her and kissed her. Smack on the lips, and it seemed that it was for more than the few seconds it actually took. One guy clapped softly. Or was it a gal? Being preoccupied at the time, Boaz could not tell nor care.

Now he had to apologize for messing up her makeup. But she did not play by his rules. Judith simply grabbed his hand, squeezed a bit, and still smiling, led him to their large dining table seating ten people. Throughout the entire meal she never uttered a word about what had just transpired. They were sitting side by side according to the little name tents. Fortuitous? Maybe. It might have had something to do with switching a tag or two a lot earlier in the evening. One does not get to be a promotion manager without learning how to promote oneself.

A heavy and rather elaborate table cloth cascaded down the sides of the large table. It interfered somewhat with the cloth napkin that etiquette taught you should cover your lap. Too much cloth. As the meal progressed from the shrimp cocktail appetizer to the clear soup of indeterminate origin, Boaz congratulated himself on picking and devouring only those dishes he felt he could enjoy. Soup was not on that list. This short pause during the fancy meal which he awaited with great anticipation, allowed him to take in the entire table busily ingesting large, liquid quantities of soup. He felt he had made the right choice. Then he felt a hand on his right knee.

Instinctively, he looked in Judith's direction. Judith sat to his right. Within the bounds of etiquette, he reached down without looking there and rearranged the bountiful cloth napkin to fully cover the space between his legs. If it also masked the movement of the hand below the napkin and the table cloth, well, he could not object to the thick folds of both, now, could he?

Boaz relaxed. The moving hand did not. It went where he knew it would. Slowly and methodically, Boaz made a detailed visual inspection of the wine glass he held. Without the benefit of the warming effect the soup provided, he began to feel uncomfortably warm. That hand knew exactly what it was doing. As Boaz thought about how to reciprocate the favor, the servers appeared to clear away the soup bowls and ask if they wanted meat or fish for their main course.

Judith, whose hand vanished from its workplace, answered for both of them by ordering fish, please as the next course. Fortunately, Boaz prefers fish to meat dishes, but it certainly did not matter, because he was not in an objecting mood.

He smiled at Judith. She smiled back. That incredible smile of hers put any thought of saying something at that point right out of his mind. The remainder of the meal continued uneventfully, except for Boaz excusing himself shortly thereafter to make a quick trip to the men's room.

The lavish meal passed the taste and presentation examination. What is not to like about a meal fit for the kings and queens of promotion? They ate and chatted and pretended to be impressed by the charming, old character actor that UBN placed at each table.

In truth, the movie matinee idol at their table was one who Boaz remembered fondly from the Saturday cowboy serials, those once-a-week chapters where you hoped in vain for the bad guys to win. Even today he could not remember his name or if he climbed on his horse as a baddie or a member of the posse. The actor spoke with fondness of those early days of talking pictures, and graciously posed with them for pictures by the roaming female photographer.

That photographer was the one who provided Boaz fifty years later with the evidence of his long-ago connection to Judith. He will always be grateful to her. As with the old character actor, she passed into history all too quickly. Boaz wished he knew her name.

Not only the famous had to leave. The time had come to depart Hollywood. The two- hundred-plus promotion managers from around the country had had their fill of indoctrination for the upcoming, new fall shows on TV. It must be added that everyone had a great time, too. Neither Judith nor Boaz could watch one more promo nor extol the virtues of the new shows they were force fed. That would come when they had returned to the real world that lay somewhere on the other side of the country.

These two young people so infatuated with each other said their good-byes the evening before flying home, once the grand meal ended at around seven-thirty, when he took her to his room at the hotel. The promotion manager with whom he shared the room they gave him had left already for whatever city he hailed from. Someone was ill in his family. That left Boaz alone for the final night in Hollywood.

With Judith's assistance, he corrected that situation. A decent bottle of chilled Sauvignon Blanc occupied a place of honor on the table with a pull-out leaf they called a desk in the room. Two glasses from the bathroom stood guard over the wine. Boaz regretted not acquiring stemmed wine glasses. Once they had closed the door, Boaz turned away so he might fiddle with the dial of the radio the hotel had so thoughtfully provided. He asked her what kind of music she would like to have play on the radio.

Whether Judith heard him or not does not matter; she was much too busy taking off her clothes and folding them, neatly, of course, over a chair. Boaz turned to face her and discovered she was way ahead of him on several fronts. Judith was naked from top to toe, and unlike him, completely at ease. He managed to put the corkscrew down just before she attacked his carefully-knotted tie.

"I can see your good looks do not end with your face. Those are two fantastic breasts," Boaz said. And that . . ." Judith interrupted him by putting her hand over his mouth. He could not tell if impatience or anger motivated her, so he shut up, because he was having trouble trying to speak through her fingers.

"Do you want to screw me, or are you just taking inventory? Aren't you going to help me?", she asked. "Men," she continued, "they simply do not know what comes first. Sex first, wine later. Give me a hand; I will not do all the work. If you're going to put your two-cents inside me, I want to get my money's worth by getting you to help undressing yourself."

Boaz was not sure he ever entirely understood her. To this day, he cannot remember how she got his clothes off. He's pretty certain he helped a bit. But that part is still too vague in his mind. She kissed him, earnestly, but without a lot of passion. Judith removed his tie quickly enough. She had some trouble with the fancy belt buckle. Yes, he did help her with that. Boaz congratulated himself on not being totally incompetent. Finally, nothing separated their bodies except a little space. The young man was beginning to catch up. His mind finally began to function. He told her she had a beautiful body as they climbed into bed.

"Will you stop with the words and prove to me you know what to do with my beautiful body," Judith demanded. This time Boaz was ready for her. He knew that to both shock and please her in the same instant he had to say something special. And he hit upon exactly the word to accomplish both reactions together.

"Are you aware that I have built my reputation on beating women? I have. But the only instrument I've ever used to beat women is my tongue. All over your body. Slowly and with love," added Boaz to prove to Judith he also knew how to use words.

He felt her instantly tense, then relax just as quickly. He had made his point. For the next ten minutes - well, maybe fifteen minutes - he drove the point home, so to speak. She came twice, he believed. Boaz held up two fingers that formed V for victory. Judith guessed he was keeping count. Her body was very damp, and both were desperately in need of a glass of wine. They drank thirstily together.

It seemed to both of them that a bottle of white wine had never disappeared so quickly. But the effort Boaz put into pouring the wine into Judith's bathroom tumbler proved shake-y at best. It spilled liberally onto her breasts. As she reached for part of the sheet to dry herself off, Boaz proved once more that he was a man of the moment.

He held her hand away from her body while making the wine vanish in a very tactile way. Judith not only did not object, she directed Boaz to a few spots she said he missed.

With the preliminaries over, real, safe penetration began. Condoms of the day lacked sophistication, and made the work more difficult. At the risk of being a bit chauvinistic, Boaz believed guys had a tougher time than gals because of that. Throughout it all, Judith said nothing . . . at least, nothing that could be defined as words. She did not have to say anything.

They were completely one, though a few seconds separated their climaxes. Their finale matched the crescendo of the music on the radio, giving Boaz the final smile on that note. Still, the good-natured exchange of words between them proved that sex can be almost as much a mental exercise as a physical one.

Neither of them had any energy left. With great effort, they pulled each other from the bed and headed toward the bathroom, where a hot shower became an immediate goal for both. They met that goal together. If one hand washes the other works for people who wish to return a favor, then that same statement can be applied to washing bodies. Tired as he was, Boaz did justice to Judith's body, and she returned the favor. Cleaned up by that quick, hot shower together, and exhausted, they lay intertwined on the bed.

"Do you mind if I finally get to say something?", he asked, as she lay in his arms. She grunted with her eyes closed. He decided it was a positive, not a negative grunt.

"You are a beautiful woman with a beautiful body."

"I thought you'd never notice," Judith murmured, turned onto her left side and promptly fell asleep. The alarm was set for two am, so Judith could return to her room on another floor in the hotel. Boaz followed her example and fell asleep also, after pulling the covers over both of them. A long and eventful day in both their lives ended on a very quiet note.

* * *

When you have to airmail yourself to the East Coast from California, chances are the plane leaves early. The moment you step onto that flight you lose three hours. Sorry, the sun moves in the wrong direction.

Boaz had some difficulty returning to the world the next morning. He was still tired and realized in a flash that Judith had responded to the two am alarm, and he had not. He glanced at the clock on the table. He was already running late to catch his airplane. Boaz surprised himself with how quickly he got ready and packed to leave.

There was no time to even make a phone call to Judith. Maybe he could make that connection at the airport. He flew, he thought, faster than the airplane he was attempting to board as he made his way to the airport that would leave Hollywood and his incredible adventure behind.

Boaz knew the airline and flight number that Judith would use, and because he left on a slightly later plane, he thought he might be able to catch up to her for a final good-bye.

Except, you see, that was not the real reason he was so anxious to see Judith once more. He wanted to be certain that she held the same feelings for him that he had for her. After knowing her for those few days, he felt unsure. She said nothing to him when she left in the middle of the previous night. He needed to talk with her one more time.

As quickly as Judith had come into his life, she was gone just as fast. And Boaz followed on his journey very soon thereafter, only in a slightly different direction.

Chapter Two

Judith Comes Home:
Atlanta, 1969

The airplane from California carrying Judith landed in Atlanta during the afternoon. With practiced momentum and agility, she weaved her car through traffic to her home north and a bit west of downtown Atlanta. She had purchased the house in an area she knew using a small inheritance. Collectively, the houses, the roads and the people felt like old friends. Judith's neighborhood was an area that gave privacy to the home where she lived. It sustained her soul.

Over the years, she poured time and money into its look and feel. She adored the sanctuary afforded by her living room, kitchen and most of all, her bedroom.

She had chosen her furniture carefully and with a mid-century modern flair. Clean, neat, uncomplicated lines echoed her own personality. A splash of color could be found in the throw pillows, the backsplash behind the sink and the huge, horribly-expensive wooden feature wall in the bedroom. The wood, along with pieces of twisted wrought iron had been fashioned into an exotic-looking headboard by a very talented artist.

Both the wood and the iron had come from an out-building on an old plantation. Judith did not know whether the materials came from a detached kitchen house or part of a slave quarters. She guessed that the wrought iron probably meant it came from a kitchen building. Otherwise, she would not have bought it.

As Judith reached her bedroom, she flung herself across her bed, partly to relax following an arduous flight she did not enjoy at all, and partly to allow herself the luxury of a few moments to relive the most intimate memory of her life. Judith had gone to bed with one or two men, but she thought of these men as boys.

Last night . . . was it only just last night, she made love with a man. More than the sex, Judith knew this might be a man she could live with forever. The several days they had together returned to her memory as delightful and tantalizing. A lot of the time they spent together was involved with work. She wished it could have been more intimate sooner. She almost knew him. Their relationship needed more time together.

During that first weekend back home, Judith shared a brunch-hour coffee with her sister, Dina. She spared no detail of her time in Hollywood, including all the promotion activity, the new man she met, and she related every detail of their lovemaking. Even something that Boaz did not know.

Dina seemed properly impressed, so much so that she paid for her younger sister's coffee. In truth, she would have paid for the coffee even without hearing those lurid details. But it made Dina feel so much closer to her sister. Paying for the coffee was simply what older sisters do.

Judith prepared to return to the TV station as a new week began on the following Monday. The upcoming fall season was her first as promotion manager. Her background included being a technical assistant at UBN, filling in on an afternoon cooking show when the female chef took ill, and taking over for the station manager's assistant when she took off time to have a baby. The station manager, Haim, liked her and decided she could replace the illiterate nephew of a news producer.

This was August, 1969 in Atlanta, the heart of the South. Most of the execs at the consistently worst-rated TV station in town felt their positions had been rubber-stamped in heaven. Their ability to do the job stretched credulity. Together, they managed to put out a barely passable daytime television product for the stay-at-home housewives of Atlanta. Fortunately, the evening programming originated with UBN. The execs were comfortable with their efforts and loved the adoration of the populace.

Into this stale mix of mediocrity came Haim, a man from the Mid-West who rose to station manager in spite of or maybe because of his name. He was Jewish. Judith knew him well through her family. Haim was not a relative, but they were attached through a common extended family connection.

There were no sexual overtones to their relationship. Distant cousins might be the best description of their relationship. Twenty-two years separated them in age. What they shared was drive and talent.

Along with Amos, a Black man who ran the department that oversaw the service personnel, these three made up what passed for tokenism at the station in the late 1960s. Amos had learned to keep his mouth shut and his eyes open. He knew his place in the structure of things. He held the job for over five years now and tolerated the incompetence around him.

Amos enjoyed being a Black executive at a TV outlet in the South's largest city. The only difference between him and the others lay in the fact that Amos knew his job and many of the other execs only thought they did.

He rather liked the still new station manager for his energy and knowledge. Refreshing was the word Amos used. That promotion lady attacked her job with the same vigor his nephew attacked his jazz guitar. "Yeah, they would do."

On the surface, tokenism passed as benevolence in a South still strictly segregated. The Civil Rights Act, which, among many other things, banned discrimination on the basis of race, color, religion, passed on the Federal level in 1963. It needed far more than six years to sink in.

By the year 1969, even the South exhibited some progress. Grudgingly. Without admitting they had done anything wrong. So companies took on a few Blacks here and there. They hired a few Jews, a couple of Mexicans, as they referred to anybody from south of the Rio Grande, and still could not decide whether to bring Catholics into the fold, based on their long-held prejudices against Papists.

The kingmakers of the South embraced tokenism to keep the Liberal Northerners quiet. Martin Luther King had been assassinated about a year-and-a-half prior to the autumn of 1969. The heat was definitely on. Atlanta, in particular, had to appear to be leading the way. With the Civil Rights Act pushing them forward, Haim and Judith went to work at the TV station. It was a small half-step forward.

Certainly they were not the only examples of tokenism in the South. But it is on them that we focus. The rumblings among the execs at the TV station never stopped. For good measure, Amos was included. The level of energy and competence rose with Haim and Judith there. It pointed out, by its very existence, that the other people at the station had less energy and far less competence. Alas, you do not make friends among your colleagues this way. Please do not try to count the number of harebrained schemes they hatched to oust this trio from their midst. Thievery, lateness, bad language, even incompetence, were posted in secret letters to the corporate offices in New York City. Curiously, the execs in the Big Apple dismissed all the complaints out of hand except one or two that showed incompetence.

It turned out that the one thing the Atlanta execs were really good at was describing incompetence. A second look separated the wheat from the chaff. Incompetence, they decided in New York City, feeds on itself. The people spreading falsehoods in Atlanta considered everything and overlooked the actual reason they would fail: tokenism.

The kingmakers had put minorities in all these companies to enhance the look of the South overall. Disgruntled executives anywhere would disturb that view. Trying to dislodge a young woman like Judith from her job would be much more difficult than it appears to be. Moreover, she was a woman. Women lacked any real representation anywhere, and that included the South. In Atlanta, she made up an army of one among promotion managers in the city, and pretty much throughout the Southern states.

Making her look bad made no sense. Getting the TV station execs to understand that took longer than it should have. But the point was made: leave her alone.

* * *

About two years before she began as promotion manager at UBN, Judith indulged one of her greatest passions by volunteering at a small farm fairly close to where she lived. The farm was run by a wealthy woman who had spent many years caring for a very ill husband. When he passed on, she turned her bountiful love and compassion to caring for animals that no one wanted. MaryLu took in chickens and goats, small primates like monkeys as well as a few old and lame horses.

But the older woman wanted to be part of the solution, not simply continue the problem. So she made her own decisions as to which animals she would care for and which to refuse.

Whatever criteria she had in mind, she did not share them with others. It meant that the animals living on the farm would be cared for for as long as they lived. That was just fine with all the animals and the volunteers who helped out.

The farm had several fruit trees and a vegetable garden, not enough to sustain the animals or bring in any money, but enough to keep the bills from adding up. The farm took donations, of course, but with the parameters MaryLu established, there were no overwhelming financial struggles.

MaryLu had thought out her enterprise quite well. When money was needed, it appeared from her purse. When love was needed, it came from a bottomless well. Just ask Jake, the old American Quarter horse with a slight limp. He and MaryLu had been together for over fourteen years. No one took care of Jake better than MaryLu. And if an extra apple or two found its way into Jake's feeding trough, not one complaint could be heard . . . especially not from Jake.

Judith left the god-playing role to MaryLu. When she spent time with the animals, she could forget about the pull-and-push of the personalities at the TV station. The equation was simple at the farm: give love, get love.

The animals did not love you less if you did not bring a carrot, but Judith had long ago decided not to press that theory. A carrot or piece of apple from the farm was always tucked into her jeans pocket. Sometimes the job was dirty, sometimes not. Judith reveled in all of it. Their love was unequivocal. She returned it.

As with all volunteers, Judith had her schedule: Four hours every Saturday, three on Sunday, and one weekday after work for as long as she could stay. The weekday trip to the farm proved to be the most difficult. Changes in the daily log of promos meant returning to the station to repair or rewrite an announcement appearing on the evening news or within a prime-time show. Occasionally, her assistant would fill in for her.

Mostly, Judith had to be there herself. These interruptions, plus an arduous workday, made up her world in television.

Complaining about them would not change a thing. So Judith never complained.

The snide remarks that filtered through to her via her few friends at the station, or passed on by her assistant, a very young boy barely out of a local college, dented, but did not penetrate her armor.

Cornelius, Judith's helper, understood schedules and numbers pretty well, but dealing with people remained out of his grasp. That can be a decided drawback when the job is public relations. He liked his boss. She treated him with kindness and more than a little compassion. When other executives phoned Judith, he would say she was busy or could not talk with them, or often, she did not want to speak to them. Cornelius believed he was protecting his boss, but he was not. If anything, it gave those who did not like her more reason to damage her reputation.

All of this recurring drama led fairly quickly to his dismissal from the station, but not before that list of callers included a man named Boaz Gluzzman. Ah, Cornelius, he froze out the one person she would have liked to speak with. Judith never knew.

Most minorities in Atlanta drew their share of entrenched hate. Women executives in the business world ended up more as curiosities than a separate workforce. You needed a magnifying glass to even notice them, let alone count them. In the early 1970s, a White, pious executive would tell you a Southern woman in a high position was not worth the spit it took to condemn her.

Outside of traditional jobs like teaching and secretarial work, women had been put on Earth to serve men in all ways. A female boss posed a contradiction-in-terms. And she was fair game for every bad joke spread throughout the city.

At the TV station, Judith focused on her her job. The swirling hate around her was barely noticed. However, hate is like a hot chili pepper: a little goes a long way. Judith kept her cool and her job over the next two-and-a-half years. A strong station manager and her low profile at UBN protected her. What she could not escape was the ratings of the daytime shows on the station lineup. Judith promoted the programs very professionally. The shows and those who produced, directed and populated them stood directly in blame's path.

You would have to be perverse to appear to shift it all onto the shoulders of the lone woman exec at the station. But the White men there were up to the task at hand.

Judith somehow bore most of the blame.

From the vantage point of many years later, Judith recalled only one time - that she could remember, when she lost her cool. It was a small incident; nothing that should have set off explosions. But it caught her with her guard down. She erupted when one of several station personnel who really thought little of women in power claimed the glass of Chardonnay she held in her hand at an office get-together actually meant she was a drunk.

Judith shot back. "You know, you're right. From that glass of red wine in your hand, I would say we are both winers, except I spell the word without an 'h'. Judith turned and walked away. The conversation had ended abruptly on a satisfying note.

Even Judith could not prevent the axe from falling. At the Easter egg party hosted each year by UBN, her closest ally, Haim, informed her that she would begin the summer unemployed.

Outwardly, Judith bore the news well. Inside, she cried, where no one could see. Her family and friends, of which she had many, grieved with her. But they had their own lives to lead. When the door closed on the last one to leave her side a few weeks later, Judith allowed herself a moment of deep, personal reflection.

She did not feel sorry for herself. She would find a way to become employed again.

But here, at the nadir point of her adult life, she allowed a picture to seep into her soul of the one man she wished she knew better: Boaz. Judith had no idea of what happened to him. Right now though, a shoulder to lean against that belonged to the one person you could have shared your life with, became the most comforting thought in her life.

It would have to remain just that: a thought.

The lady had work to do. She needed a plan. A direction. A theme. A new life. Judith pondered while alone with the animals on the farm. She certainly had extra time for them now. They patiently waited while she explored various media and writing jobs within her qualifications. It was a fair exchange. Judith spoke with the chickens and the horses, and they received a handful of grain or a carrot for listening. But she kept running up against the barriers most women had to deal with in the 1970s. No one ever took their executive qualifications seriously enough to employ them.

Mirabelle the goat showed great compassion for the woman holding the carrot. But Mirabelle was not an employer of other women. But maybe, thought Judith, she could be.

She let the idea percolate in her head for a few minutes. Picking herself up from the bench where she sat with Mirabelle's head resting on her leg, Judith sought out MaryLu in the kitchen of the large home at the end of the field.

"If you have a moment," Judith queried, "I have an idea."

The huge salad MaryLu was preparing would have to wait a short while longer. She returned it to the fridge so she might give this earnest volunteer her complete attention. She liked Judith. Judith fell into that category of human beings who understood the significance and value of animals, so it was just possible that she had something important to say.

They sat themselves on the sunny porch adjacent to the kitchen. Each woman had fortified herself with a frosty glass of iced tea, to which MaryLu added a plate of her home-baked cookies. In this perfect summer setting, Judith added her perfect idea.

"I think the animals on the farm should earn their keep," she began. "Let's put them to work. Every weekend in a designated area, we can have a petting zoo," offered Judith, adding, "though I don't like the word zoo. A petting park. Yes, a petting park. Suppose we call it Jake's Petting Park. We could charge admission. The money would go toward buying food for the animals. Some of the volunteers could give talks about how to care for specific animals. And, at the end, each kid feeds one animal — under supervision, of course."

MaryLu put down her glass carefully so as not to spill a drop of the ice-cold tea, got up and went to where Judith waited in anticipation, bent over and kissed her on the cheek.

"Honey-Child, you had me at *Jake's Petting Park*. How did you get so smart? Work out a plan on paper and submit it to me by . . . how long do you need?"

"I need a week to establish food quantities, times, setup costs, and some graphics for a brochure. Is that too long," asked Judith?

"No," replied MaryLu, "it's probably too short a time. Take two weeks and do it right. I will pay you a decent sum. If I really like what you propose, I will make sure you are happy, too."

So that is how Judith's second career as an event planner began. About the only one who might have objected, Mirabelle, got an extra carrot or two for putting the idea in Judith's head. The suddenly-busy young woman apologized profusely to Mirabelle because she named the park after a male and not her. In times of stress, even Judith could succumb to expediency.

Over the next two weeks, the plan took shape. Judith was in her element. She called in a few favors from artist friends of hers and got a logo and a brochure developed. She ran the nitty-gritty figures for MaryLu and was pleasantly surprised by how much they would clear as profit over the first year. With small startup costs, those once-neglected animals would be on a steak-and-champagne diet before the end of the first year.

Hyperbole aside, the park brought in youngsters and their families by the many hundreds through the first year alone. Judith even approached the local elementary schools to add Jake's Park for class trips. It became too successful. Eventually, MaryLu had to impose her own, mysterious limits on school visits. But the volunteers and the animals loved the extra attention they received.

They would have gladly put up a plaque in Judith's honor if they had had more than a few dollars in expendable income between them. Everyone was certain the animals would have contributed also, if carrots could be converted to cash. Judith might have approved. Maybe.

MaryLu proved to be more than generous to Judith. She spread the word among her friends that she knew of a creative woman who could plan and execute complicated agendas like parties, weddings, prom parties, Bar/Bat Mitzvas, and a host of other events that the well-off folks in the suburbs of Atlanta conjured up to amuse and beguile their friends.

Judith built the event-planning business through her hard work. She rented a small, chic office in a new area north of downtown Atlanta. The work load had created a full-time job for a second person. During these early days of building her business reputation, Judith actually got to plan an Easter egg party. She used the occasion to hire a new assistant, which she saw as a fitting repayment for the same occasion that the station used to fire her. Judith was not above *getting even*.

Her assistant was a no-nonsense young woman fresh out of college. Laura was creative, smart, out of work and very Puerto Rican. From the looks of her, Laura had enough Black blood coursing through her veins to pass for either Latina or Black. Her ability on her own as a minority to occupy such a position in the Deep South during those days ran from nil to none.

Working for Judith gave her an opportunity she would not have had. Together they solidified and built the business over the next nine years. Laura's enthusiasm and intellectual skills grew to match Judith's. The business thrived.

There were, of course, other examples throughout the South and in Atlanta of White folks helping minorities. One wonders how many hands you would need to count them. The point is, any such count would have to include Judith.

Almost a decade later, a more mature and experienced Laura left then to open her own event-planning business in the heart of downtown Atlanta. The times were indeed changing. She named her event-planning business Mirabelle, a name she knew Judith would approve of, and to try to repay Judith for hiring her for her first job.

During those years when the business moved under its own momentum, Judith found time to pen several short stories about her favorite animal, Mirabelle. She truly enjoyed writing. After her years in television, she missed the creativity that came with promoting the television station. Composing proposals for clients' events just did not hold the same challenge for her brain.

So Judith took to writing about *Marvelous Mirabelle, the Miracle-Working Goat*. Those exploits covered almost two dozen not-very-long stories in which a goat saves the day. It allowed Judith to present a goat's view of the world as the bearded lady expounded on climate, human frailties and even love.

Most of all, Mirabelle was given a much better alliterative name than *Jake's Petting Park*. In this way, Judith felt she finally honored her beloved, old friend.

Life was slowly improving for women in the South. A new assistant occupied Laura's place in Judith's business. Another Latina woman, because Judith could not find a man she could accept. Nellie was a hard worker, but less creative than Laura. By then, the business had developed its own impetus, and pretty much coasted along.

The energy level of Judith's youth dropped, and she spent less time seeking new projects, although she still loved creating interesting and well-planned events for her clientele. The years were passing. Without actually being aware of time, Judith saw the twenty-first century come into being. She aged into her sixties as a successful woman.

Although Judith had resigned herself to look past the hate toward minorities that was woven into the hearts of so many in the South, she could never accept it. She added her voice and walked in marches that brought her to other Southern cities. By comparison, Atlanta exhibited a few degrees more progressiveness than the small towns and even cities throughout the South. But it did not help.

Hate was hate, wherever it reared its head. Blacks bore the brunt of it. They always did, but especially in the South. Other minorities also caught their share of the hate. Judith, herself a member of a minority, at last began to wonder what it might be like to live in the North.

She had never entertained such a thought. Now, older and a bit wiser, she let her mind wander to different places. She thought of Philadelphia, where Boaz was born, and of Buffalo where he lived. She had never been to New York City, or Boston, Chicago or who-knows-where-else in the North. The Travel Bug had bitten Judith.

Chapter Three

Judith on the Road North: September, 2012

Aside from those protest marches in the South, it had been years since a trip anywhere had nudged its way onto her social calendar. Nellie was competent enough to run the office if the work load stayed at the level to which it had fallen as Judith aged. It freed Judith to work out a travel plan.

Since she could only count a few places she might check off her extensive list of where to go, the problem for Judith lay in an overabundance of vacation venues. Money presented no problem, but decisions did. She spent about two weeks with maps and plans. In the end, she knew a great deal about places and still had no concrete itinerary.

Judith did not like to fly in an airplane. She decided to drive north directly up the Interstate highways that connected Georgia to Massachusetts. She gave herself two weeks to reach New England, where Cape Cod beckoned. On the way, she thought small side trips to places like New York City and Washington, DC seemed appealing.

Judith knew she would not be able to bypass a day or two in Philadelphia, though she was reluctant after so many years without Boaz to mention out loud why the city drew her to itself. New York City and Providence would lead her to Boston and the Cape.

The return trip needed no stopovers, except to sleep.

Judith reckoned that she would be back in her cozy Atlanta home in three weeks. The lady knew how to plan. On a relatively mild summer day in September, 2012, she said her good-byes and drove off on her new adventure.

The long trip ahead of her allowed Judith to begin to relax and think. Almost in spite of herself, she began to review where life had taken her. She reviewed in her mind the business she had begun because a little goat had spoken to her. Oh, Judith knew that was not truly the case; she needed luck and more than a little help along the way. She took a moment to thank MaryLu for buying into her idea of a petting park. Then there was Laura, who really helped her build a very solid business. Judith silently wished her well at her *Mirabelle* planning business in the downtown area.

It was going to be a long, relaxing trip, and she put aside such specific thoughts for a while as she turned her attention to the passing landscape, accompanied by the classical music on the radio.

Judith drove in a direct line from Atlanta, straight through to Charlotte, North Carolina, arriving just after lunchtime. She parked at a charming restaurant. After lunch, she drove around

Charlotte to get a feel of it, then continued driving north. On the road just outside Greensboro, NC, she stopped at a quaint local inn for the night.

The woman in charge, a pleasant-looking Black lady, greeted her warmly and once the formalities were over, showed her to a lavishly-decorated room. It made Judith wonder whether the American Civil War happened in the past or lay ahead in the future. Her rental was study in excess.

Billowy drapes containing oversized floral patterns and intricately-patterned wall paper screamed luxury from a world that once prized such ostentatiousness. The furniture and scattered *chachkas* paid homage to the curved lines that the rich of another era thought announced their wealth to the world. Judith wallowed in this look of the Old South. Although the apartment did not even approach her taste, she permitted the decor to envelop her completely for this one night.

The night, however, remained elusive. The woman who checked her in had a story to tell and invited her newest lodger for a cup of tea and some cake. She turned out to be the owner of the inn and at the end of a long, quiet day relaxed with Judith. The tale she told exploded in Judith's mind because it hit very close to her heart.

Sleep would play an insignificant role in the immediate hours that lay before her.

Christina, so named because she came into this world close to, but not exactly on Christmas, had graduated from a college that specialized in how to care and feed tourists. Her rapport with travelers came naturally to her, and Christina enjoyed her work. She quickly realized she knew better than most how to run a hotel. But she put in her years learning the intricacies of the business, not to mention dealing with the disgust most White folks in the travel world had for Blacks with a brain in their head.

The lady put up with it all, and quietly, deliberately, saved her money. For years, it had been her dream to own a place of her own for travelers. As with everything else in her life, she would have to accomplish it relying just on herself, with some help from her husband. Christina invested wisely and in several years' time put together enough money for this small, out-of-the-way inn. It was all hers.

Ideas poured out of her mature head. She told Judith how she fought the town and the town supervisors to upgrade the laws that they themselves flaunted. Christina proved tougher and smarter than the innkeepers and many of the lawmakers in the area.

Slowly, she showed them how to improve tourist travel. Travelers began stopping overnight at *Your Antique Belle* outside Greensboro and spending money in the city. Christina's success was colored green, as in dollars spent liberally in Greensboro.

They did not bother her very much once Christina's ideas helped with everyone's profits. Even on a slow day like today, the people in Greensboro knew that the tourists would return next weekend. Black women do not receive the credit they often deserve, and Christina was no exception to this rule in a White world.

But truly, Christina had a bigger hole in her life that she needed to fill. If Judith wanted another cup of tea and a home-made coffee cake, that story was a whistle of the kettle away. Judith accepted the offer, and by doing so, called into being a story that struck at her heart as much as it had tormented Christina for all of her life.

"Do you run this marvelous inn all by yourself," asked Judith. "You must have at least fifty apartments. I suppose they have been outfitted with same care and lavish attention to detail as my room."

"Actually, we have 62 rooms. A few have long-term tenants, older folk mostly, with a some money and nowhere to go. They like the atmosphere. They're off in one wing of the building where they seem to enjoy each other's company. This evening, only a few travelers have taken to the highways. So I have time to relax with a nice lady."

The tea and cake appeared. And Christina warmed to the telling of her story. Judith was completely unprepared for its impact on her. They sat in an adequate breakfast nook off the small lobby that delivered food in a decidedly more modern setting.

"Of course I have staff," continued Christina. "Also, my husband, Zeke, runs a financial advising company in town. He helps me with the books, though I'm quite capable of doing it alone. Still, I love him very much and enjoy working together with him.

We have two kids. Kathy, our daughter, who is fresh out of the same college that I attended, helps when she's not at school teaching high schoolers with developmental problems. Noam is a lot younger than Kathy. He's a teenager growing up. Boys take a bit longer to develop than girls do. I'm quite sure there's a very talented human being and musician hidden inside him that will emerge soon."

As they sipped the recently-brewed tea, both women readied themselves for the tale one would tell and the other react to. The twenty-first century was only in its teenage years. Judith realized again what she had seen while marching in Southern towns with local Blacks: they lived their lives not greatly different than Whites, with pretty much the same hopes for themselves and their loved ones as Whites had.

True, their fears were different, magnified by centuries of hate and inequality. It changed their lives. How could it not?

Judith felt close to this middle-aged woman who she knew for about an hour. But even she could not realize how close. That discovery was almost an hour into the future.

"As much time and effort that I spent establishing this inn, this dream of mine for many years, I decided to turn away from interacting with the lawmakers of Greensboro and concentrate on the one thing missing from my life throughout my entire life. You see, I don't know who my father is," concluded Christina.

"Sometime in the early 1960s, my mother had sex with a White man. She said it was consensual. I'm not so sure that it was. Anyway, mama would not tell me who my father was. As I grew old enough to add emphasis to the question, my mama grew older refusing to answer me. This game - can I even call it a game - went on until mama died in 1993. She took her secret with her to her grave.

"But mama didn't understand what a determined daughter she had. What little I knew was mostly what she had told me, or let slip. My young mind would wrap itself around every scrap of information. And never let go. No, never."

As she told her story, Christina's passion grew. The tea, on the other hand, grew cold. With a start, she understood what had happened. She quickly made the two of them a fresh pot of tea. The tea cooled; Christina's passion calmed. And the tale continued.

"Mama worked for the man who bedded her as a sales lady in a haberdashery store. The man owned the store. Mama said he treated her well and paid for everything related to the birth. But he swore mama to secrecy. I know it was the early 1960s, but we're talking about me. I do not like being someone's afterthought, someone's inconvenient outcome, a difficult ending to an easy conquest. I am me, and I'm smart.

"And what everyone seems to overlook, I'm half White: I understand White folks. "Don't mis-understand, Judith. I am proud to be Black. Being Black is my life and my kids' lives. My heritage and my color won't wash off. Don't want it to.

But there exists a piece of my life that I can't see or touch. That certainly bothers me more than the self- righteous lawmakers in this town."

Judith was hooked on Christina's story. The questions that Christina must have asked herself began to form in Judith's mind. She ventured to ask her first question, "Where did this happen in Greensboro?"

"Oh, we're not talking about North Carolina," Christina answered. "In those days, mama lived in Philadelphia. That's where I was born. Mama moved here just after I became an inconvenient fact. Whoever he was paid for the move. Mama and me skedaddled South. We were gone like we never existed."

Christina lowered her voice in a conspiratorial fashion. She said that as she grew up she would pump mama for information. Mama kept her word to that man in Philadelphia, but she was no match for her increasingly inquisitive daughter.

One day, she let slip his last name: Gluzzman. It did not help. By then, Christina discovered, there were no Gluzzmans still alive and living in Philadelphia.

Judith froze. She knew someone with that name. Carefully, she prepared herself for her next question, "With two Zs?"

It was Christina's turn to freeze. "Yeah. Mama said that. How do you know?"

"At a time long ago, in a far-away place that everybody calls Hollywood, I met a man called Gluzzman. We were both young and fell in love - at least I believe we did - and then we went separate ways. It happened very fast. Over a few days in, let's see, 1969. When I knew him, he lived in upstate New York, in Buffalo. But his family," Judith added, "came from Philadelphia."

To say that Christina was surprised and fascinated would be an understatement. Meanwhile, Judith's mind went off in many directions as Boaz entered her thoughts once more. Christina interrupted; she wanted to know more.

With considerable effort, Judith dragged her thoughts back to the empty tea cups, the crumb-filled plates . . . and reality. Briefly, she retold the story of their finding each other at the promotion managers' meeting, only leaving out the really good parts.

Then, she excused herself and went to sleep for a few hours. A long drive lay ahead.

Pen and paper had already appeared in Christina's hand as she wrote notes to herself. These leads would fill her days and a few nights over the next few weeks. It took several months for Christina to resolve where her investigation took her. As with her other investigations, it all came to nothing. She never found her father. Still, her conversation with Judith had provided a few tangible hints that she had never had. She wrote a long, heart-felt letter of thanks to Judith for her help.

But Judith never received it.

By the late morning of the second day, Judith reached the nation's capital. The massive and impressive buildings that make up Washington, D.C. held little to no interest for her. She drove around the city just to see the face of America to the world.

Imposing as the buildings are, she saw them as cold, unfeeling monuments to power, prestige and the inevitable hatred that has spilled from them onto every state in the Union. With a shudder, Judith drove away.

North of Washington, DC, she continued on until Baltimore, MD. Just outside the city, she stopped for the night at a small, local motel. Judith was not feeling well, so she decided not to push on to Philadelphia. A short dinner and bed were all that remained on her agenda for that day. Judith was thankful there was no storyteller at this motel. She had enjoyed her visit with Christina and wondered what it must be like to have no inkling of who your father might be. It remained beyond her imagination this evening.

The drive to Philly went quickly. She decided to choose a hotel in the historical area, close to the Delaware river. That way, she could walk wherever she wished. Upon checking in, the hotel clerk noticed that she was from Atlanta. He directed her to a small, historical sign a few blocks away along the waterfront. When Judith went there after seeing the Liberty Bell, she saw that she had finally left the South.

The sign announced to the world that this was the beginning of *The Mason-Dixon Line*.

MASON-DIXON SURVEY
Here, in 1763, the southernmost point of
Philadelphia was determined as the starting point for the survey of one of the
most important borders in the nation.
Charles Mason and Jeremiah Dixon took
scientific measurements of a degree of
latitude, elevating professional surveying
standards. The survey ended a land dispute
begun by William Penn and Lord Baltimore.
Western Pa. Indian wars and severe weather
delayed completion of the line until 1768.
PENNSYLVANIA HISTORICAL AND MUSEUM COMMISSION 2013

Judith had no idea where Boaz might be in Philadelphia . . . or anywhere, for that matter. Being in his city gave her a connection with him. Beyond that link, the city had a certain warmth and historical feel. She would not be able to explore that path on this visit, but she tucked a visit to Philly into the back of her mind for a future trip.

She returned to the hotel early and went straight to bed, not taking the time to think about dinner. She did not feel well. A long, fitful night of sleep in small snatches were all she could look forward to this time. The next morning Judith left on the approximately ninety-mile drive to The Big Apple.

Judith could not say she had never been to New York City. Vaguely, she remembered visiting there as a child. She resisted going there later in life, because she had always felt comfortable with her Southern surroundings. Even her trips as promotion manager in Atlanta to view the upcoming fall shows at UBN on the West Coast tore her out of her comfort zone. So being in The Big Apple was new to her in that sense.

The desk clerk in Philly had kindly directed her to the nearby bridge, which put her quickly onto the New Jersey Turnpike and straight north to the Holland Tunnel. As she emerged into mid-town Manhattan, the enormity of the high-rises she encountered overwhelmed her. Many high-rise buildings stood in the South and the West, but never in this quantity or seemingly, this high.

Driving aimlessly through this labyrinth of sunless concrete, Judith sought a place to park. It did not exist for her.

She was exhausted and hungry. By chance, she found herself on the Avenue of the Americas where most of the communication industry headquarters could be found — including UBN. She drove past, craning her neck in a vain effort to see the top of the building. She drove on.

Eventually, Judith stopped at a parking lot near the East River. It was a seedy neighborhood. A pleasant-looking luncheonette beckoned just outside the lot. She brushed aside her fears and entered. Sitting on a stool at one of the several islands jutting out to accommodate more patrons, Judith slowly relaxed and refreshed herself, eating a bit more than she should have and not caring at all.

She actually enjoyed the food. Of course, when you are starving, all food seems good. Yet as she gave it *a second thought*, Judith had to admit her Reuben sandwich was truly enjoyable. Her waitress proved to be pleasant and helpful. Upon hearing the sad story Judith told her about being lost in New York City — one that she had, no doubt, heard many times, she proved that New Yorkers are compassionate and directed this lost soul to the Brooklyn Bridge not far away and from there to Brooklyn Heights.

Here Judith would find a trendy neighborhood with charming brownstones of reasonable size. It looked back on Manhattan from the other side of the East River. In the Heights, the world returned to its normal proportions. She found a small hotel and went directly to sleep. So deeply did she sleep that checkout time came and went.

When she met with the clerk, the lady proved to be the owner and forgave her an extra- day's rent. She too, had heard every story from and about wayward travelers. The owner joined the waitress from yesterday in showing that New Yorkers really do understand the people that they come in contact with.

Following the owner's directions, Judith recrossed the Brooklyn Bridge. She loved that old bridge. In no time at all, the Jersey Turnpike loomed in from of her, and she had to decide whether to go north or south.

She never made it to Cape Cod. As the first week progressed past its halfway point, she experienced such terrific pain in her gut, she turned south and headed home to Atlanta. The realization that she was abandoning her well-planned trip north hardly registered on her conscious mind. Pain had put out all other thoughts from her head. She drove slowly and deliberately.

Judith did not tolerate incompetence in driving, not even from herself.

Chapter Four

The Journey Ends: Atlanta, 2013

Somewhere near Charlotte, in North Carolina, Judith violated her own rule; she was paying attention more to the pain in her body than the road ahead of her. She made a perfectly safe and wrong turn without realizing it and continued driving for over thirty-five minutes.

What jarred her senses back to reality was an overhead traffic listing of the upcoming towns containing names that were unknown to her, except one: Statesville. Now why was that one familiar?

It bothered Judith so much that she pulled off the road and into the parking lot of a bland and unimpressive strip mall that was more convenient than appealing. As she thought about it, Judith realized two things: her map said she was traveling in the wrong direction; and the town named Statesville claimed its place in history as the site where a young, ex-Confederate soldier with the moniker of Tom Dula was hanged. The story gushed like a torrent of water into her thoughts, as she remembered the tale told by her earnest, but unpredictable assistant at the TV station, Clarence.

Clarence loved folk tales and the songs that were often associated with them. He would regale Judith with folk tales of fervent love and horrible death. Stories of death intrigued him most. And he enjoyed telling Judith of the Statesville hanging.

It was a convoluted tale. Most home-grown stories are; or else, why tell them? The young man who paid with his life for the killing of a woman was ultimately judged by history to be innocent. Another woman who he knew escaped that judgment, but not the guilty part. Tom Dula chose to die for the woman he loved, the actual killer. The woman who was murdered seems to have been the victim of her jealousy. It is a tale told thousands of times in both song and story.

Judith turned the car in the other direction as soon as she could do it safely. She retraced her path back toward the main road that would bring her home to Atlanta. Without being even conscious she was singing it, a song based on this story of a shortened life filled Judith's voice with apprehension, but she had no idea why. The song, according to Clarence, came out of these unfortunate circumstances and was made famous many years later.

For reasons that Judith understood to be connected to its pronunciation, the spelling of the name of the young man at the end of the noosed rope was changed to Tom Dooley.

Suppressing an involuntary shudder as best she could - death seemed so close, Judith all of a sudden saw the road sign appear that would take her south once more toward home. Her mind had occupied itself with the gruesome story so much that for a short time she forgot her own pain.

Slowly, Judith finally began to notice the familiar vegetation of the South. Four days into the return trip she pulled into her driveway. She had alerted Dina, her older sister, and her niece, Esty with a pay phone call when she was less than a day out of Atlanta.

They stood in front of her home as she joined them. Esty, and her husband, Max, put Judith into their car and they sped to the hospital.

A long night of many tests probed her seventy-one-year-old body, as a growing number of friends and relatives gathered in the eerie, dark halls. By mid-morning of the following day, a kind, old and very tired-looking head physician found all three asleep on the couch. The doctor took Dina and Esty aside and pronounced the verdict: advanced pancreatic cancer.

Judith, he told them, had not taken good care of herself. He could find no record of her cancer in her medical records. But it was also true that she had not had a checkup for quite a long, long time.

Judith would need continuous care. The hospital would do what it could, but home care in a familiar environment was the best treatment. Perhaps the only useful treatment at this stage. As the chief physician in Judith's case and his aides and nurses told them over the next few hours, the cancer was about to win the battle during the coming weeks and possibly months.

Hospital care at this point would be costly and ultimately useless in her case. It was their decision as Judith's closest relatives on the course of action that should be taken. True, the doctor felt obligated to mention putting Judith in a hospice. Neither woman would hear of it. In their mind, a hospice meant you were destitute; no one wanted you.

They conferred and decided their decision was no longer one of life or death; it was only a determination of how Judith would die. Judith, they decided, would pass from this world as she had lived till this point: fighting. And they would fight with her.

Armed with detailed instructions on how to make Judith comfortable, mother and daughter attacked the situation as only loving relatives can. While Judith remained coherent, they suggested strongly that she sell her lovely home and move in with Esty and Max located not far away.

Judith had almost no struggle left in her, and under Dina's watchful eye, the house of her dreams that gave her personality physical expression was sold for a good price. How is it that people pour so much effort and love into their physical surroundings, that when it must change - as Judith's did so abruptly, we equate it to losing an old friend or even a loved one. And yet, change it did.

The transition to the large home occupied by Esty and Max took several trips. Judith required only a modest amount of space for her clothes and the bric-a-brac of a lifetime. A few days later, Judith had a new home.

That left only one major detail of Judith's life that needed to be settled. The business created and lovingly grown had to be disposed of. Just one buyer came forward, and she exhibited Judith's same passion for the business, because it was she who gave life along with Judith herself to creating that entity. Laura expanded to a second Mirabelle office when she purchased the business from Judith a month after that. Her debt to Judith could now be marked *Paid in Full.*

Time passes very slowly when you need only count days. Whatever medications that were prescribed were lovingly administered by Esty. No one, she decided, was going to care for her aunt other than she and her mother. It was her mission of mercy and love. Even without formal nursing skills, Esty devoted herself to her aunt over the two months since Judith moved in with them. It was a losing battle.

Esty knew that, but she would not be deterred. Morning and night, she administered to her aunt's needs. As Judith weakened, Esty grew stronger. No task, however small, stood in her way. Esty would fight Judith's last battle with her and for her.

Judith lay back on the bed in her room at her niece's home. It was a large four-poster in an expansive room. She pushed the small meal of cereal away, confident that she could confine food to a category that no longer contained the words, *necessary to sustain life.* She was tired of fighting. Still, she tried to concentrate. Memories came in little patches and invaded her thoughts in a random order.

Delirium had set in. Judith flitted from the farm to her office at UBN Television to the parties she had planned and the decorations she had cut by hand. Could it be that she was losing her grasp on reality? The answer to that question remained beyond her as her niece came in to clear the small dish and spoon that might be called dinnerware on the tiny table next to the bed.

Suddenly, Judith had a thought. With what passed for excitement, she urged her beloved niece to put down the tray she carried and come close so Judith could speak almost directly into her ear.

"Have you ever been beaten, Esty? I have. It was wonderful sex. I never had an experience like that since. I felt love that day like never before. Never. Never. Never. I really loved that man with all my heart." In her delirium, Judith neglected to add that Boaz beat her using only his tongue.

The horror on Esty's face contrasted with the most magnificent smile taking over all of Judith's visage. "Beaten?," her niece said out loud. She could not believe what her aunt had just uttered. Judith personified the fighter, the gentle lover of children and animals, the leader among women. "Beaten," escaped Esty's lips for the second time. She looked down on her aunt in complete disbelief. For a second that lasted an eternity, she stared at the absolutely beautiful smile on her aunt's face. Only a very few can command the ability to light up all around them with such a pervasive smile. Judith always had that ability.

Finally, it occurred to her to ask what circumstances led up to this terrible act. But Esty stopped in mid sentence. Judith had died.

Great tears poured from her eyes. She screamed. Members of the family and friends who had gathered specifically because they were told Judith's end was approaching, rushed into the bedroom within seconds. Esty's husband, Max, grabbed her and held her tight. Of the half-dozen or so who burst in, everyone who saw Judith commented on the smile still fixed on her face. It would disappear slowly as her muscles relaxed in death. But not before it was seen and discussed by all . . . except Esty.

Esty was indeed overcome by grief. That required no play-acting on her part. She could not, however, participate in the talk about the beautiful smile on Judith's face. So she allowed her tears to speak for her without having to say anything. She resolved at this momentous moment that this would become the family's most closely-guarded secret. Esty would tell no one why Judith smiled in death. Not her husband. Not her best friend. Not even her mother. Well, maybe her mother, Judith's older sister.

And so, Judith had died, which should have been the end of it all, but that was definitely not the case. Judith would continue to have an impact on the lives of those she had loved, and as it turned out, even more of an impact on those who loved her. The family buried their adored relative in a cemetery with no tombstones. Small plaques identified the occupants of the graves. Manicured grass and sculptured lakes defined the landscape of Eternal Gardens. It was indeed a beautiful, final resting place in Atlanta.

* * *

Life moved on for everyone in the family, except Judith, of course, and Esty. The burden of the secret she carried ate at Esty's insides. She had sworn herself to secrecy. No one could know of her aunt's . . . *aberration*, Esty called it. But she had to tell someone, and that someone had to be her mother.

So, on a clear, sunny day in the late summer, about a month after Judith was laid to rest, she invited her mother for coffee at a cafe they both loved. It was one of those days when the world seemed to be moving gently in the right direction, or so Esty thought. Whatever excuse filled her mind, it proved to be enough to coax Esty into spilling the truth about her aunt.

About twenty minutes into their get-together, Esty took Lady Macbeth's advice, *screwed her courage to the sticking place* and blurted out what happened during Judith's last minutes alive. Dina's expression told her daughter nothing during the minute or two it took for Esty to unburden herself. No reaction. Although, she did ask her daughter to repeat the word beat, more as a question than a statement. When Esty finished, the younger woman looked confused. She asked her mother what she thought of Judith's love of being beaten. Dina's answer, when it finally came out, was epic . . . in emphasis, in brevity, in cutting to the heart of the question. She laughed uncontrollably.

Her coffee spilled, the dainty cakes she loved so much went flying. Dina stood up and brushed herself off as the waitress came scurrying over to mop and clean. The two women drew all the attention from the lunchtime crowd. Any thought that Esty had about keeping this a private, quiet conversation was brusquely brushed aside by her mother's uproar. They were the center of attention in the pink and blue coffee shop where the two of them had spent much time and even more money.

"Give me a moment, darling," urged her mother as she stood and finished brushing away crumbs and coffee stains. "I'm sorry. I just could not believe how you misinterpreted the situation. But you're not to blame. That beautiful sister of mine managed to screw things up, right up to her very end. And you bought into it. Let me sit down, and I will tell you a story."

And that is what Dina proceeded to do. From the beginning to the end, she retold the story of that after-dinner love session, exactly as Judith had told her originally. That is how Esty finally learned that the beatings administered by Boaz were only done with his tongue. At first, Esty's eyes widened. That was followed by a snort, then a laugh, then she pounded the table top twice. The two ladies at the next table decided to pay their bill and leave. The pink and blue coffee shop was no longer a haven for proper people.

"Wow. I feel terrible that I doubted Aunt Judith. I so loved and admired her. She wanted to tell me the whole story, but she couldn't. Wow. What an exit line. I just wish I knew to applaud when it happened."

Esty corrected that oversight by standing up in the coffee shop and applauding enthusiastically. A few coffee drinkers, not knowing what this was all about, joined in with their applause. Esty called out, "Thank you for applauding my aunt." Of course, it was her mother who was sitting next to Esty, not her aunt, but trying to explain that to those cooperative coffee drinkers would have only added to the confusion. So neither Esty nor her mother even tried.

Dina said, "Let's get out of here while the crowd is with us." They paid the bill, and as they left, Dina added, "I forgot to tell you that your Aunt Judith mentioned to me she had three orgasms, not two, before regular sex. She never told him, because she didn't want him to get a swelled head." Esty chuckled out loud for all to hear. In fact, she continued to laugh all the way home in spite of herself and did not care who heard her.

Dina paused as the two of them left the pink and blue coffee shop and asked no one in particular, "I wonder, is he still alive?"

Chapter Five

Boaz Comes Home: Buffalo, 1969

The airplane from California carrying Boaz landed in Buffalo during the afternoon.

While the actual descent to the airport went quite normally, Boaz would later look upon it as the beginning of his descent into Hell. His return to this city, which held such promise for his future, set off a series of events that, simply put, changed his life completely. Boaz would forever describe them as *hateful.*

It began almost immediately. He called the woman he had been seeing to say he had arrived. Other than that simple piece of information, he never got much further in his introductory conversation.

"You told my father that *we were getting married,*" screamed Sandy, so loud that Boaz had to hold the pay phone handle slightly away from his ear. He waited until a few more less-than-pleasant words that only remotely resembled sentences escaped her lips before venturing an answer.

"It was a joke," he confessed. "I only wanted him to feel good about our relationship. He had been very stressed about you. He did not tell me why, but I think I know why now. So I said that *we might be getting married. I never said we were getting married.*"

"Boaz, you're an idiot. My father will *never see the difference* between *what might happen* and *what will happen* when you are talking about me. You have put me into a position where I feel I must do something. So I intend to. I have taken a job in another city, and *you will not know where that is.* I'm leaving Buffalo. Most of all, Boaz, *I am getting you the hell out of my life.*

"This past week while you were away has been unbearable for me," Sandy continued. "My father . . . and even my mother won't let me alone. *Some parts of my life I do not share with them. I can't take it anymore.* They have descended on me as if I were Helen of Troy and had to be saved. I leave tomorrow. *Don't come to see me. Don't call. Don't do anything, Boaz, except contemplate how you have screwed up my life.*"

The phone abruptly clicked off. Portable phones of a later era do not permit slamming, an oversight that causes frustration on one end and confusion on the other. A lot can be said about those old, bulky dial phones. Most of it is critical. However, slamming the receiver down at the appropriate moment offers a deeply satisfying finale to a difficult conversation. Sandy got hers from her dial phone. Moreover, her satisfaction eventually grew based on the fact that it was the last time she ever spoke to Boaz.

A very confused and angry young man hung up the pay phone in the Buffalo airport. All he could think of at this moment had to do with Sandy's penchant for quoting history in the middle of a sentence. Sandy Bloom was one of the smartest women he had met in his young life. He had been attracted to her when they met while working in the local Community Theater. He really liked her.

Love? Not a word he used with Sandy. Getting close to her became increasingly difficult during the few months he had known her. Their relationship was platonic; that is the way Sandy wanted it to be. Boaz began to suspect the reason why less than a month into knowing her. He came to the conclusion she was a lesbian.

Remember that the U.S. had reached the fall of 1969 without having to deal openly with gays and lesbians. Their time would come, but by the raucous end of that decade, the approach to sexual thought of the average person had only begun to loosen. The influence of events such as the Woodstock Concert that August jangled the stereotypes in the minds of many people. They still had to learn what those terms meant. *Even today that is true.*

In 1969, Boaz knew what the words gay and lesbian signified. It did not help. His problem lay in the fact that, while he had nothing in particular against gays or lesbians, most people did. If people at work discovered he had been seeing a lesbian, it could affect his reputation at the station.

Boaz believed, and has always believed, that there are no secrets. Everything you want to keep to yourself will come out. And that part of the equation really scared him.

Sandy hid her feelings well. She knew she had to hide the way she felt even including enjoying a seemingly serious relationship with a man. Boaz had walked right into that situation. He realized this was only speculation on his part. However, going away as he did for close to a week can clear up a lot of the smoke and distortion from mirrors clouding your vision. He convinced himself Sandy was a lesbian, and he was a sacrificial Joan of Arc.

"My goodness," Boaz thought, "I'm even beginning to talk like her." Reacting to his deep and impassioned anger of the moment, he decided to put all thoughts of Sandy . . . *and all women out of his mind. Even Judith.* He harbored doubts about her, also. He had tried to call her at the station. For reasons he could not understand, he did not get the chance to speak with her. After a few tries, he gave up. Perhaps, as the young man on the phone told him, she really did not wish to speak with him. Maybe it was time to forget her.

Boaz had not planned on being so attracted to Judith. Even more surprising, he had not foreseen the connection they would have over such a short time. It certainly conflicted with his relationship with Sandy. Truth to tell, it about ended it.

Sandy's reaction upon his coming home to Buffalo did indeed turn Boaz off to her.

And so began a rejection *that came to color the rest of his life*. Little decisions. We make them all the time: from what to eat for breakfast to what to say or do in any given moment of upheaval. They appear innocuous when first uttered, because they are, but when we attach too much importance to them, these small turns in the road can lead us astray. We may pay a price far in excess of that decision.

Boaz whipped his anger into fury as he made his way out of the airport and drove to his home in suburban Buffalo. He was a good driver, but it took all of his concentration to reach his apartment this afternoon.

To his way of thinking, he had been used to cover up another person's approach to life. He did not give a damn about whether she was or was not a lesbian. "Live and let live" had always been a motto of his. But he felt used, even abused, by her. And that annoyed him. Would his reaction have been so strong if she had not been a lesbian? Well, probably not. It would take a very long time before he could even try to answer that question objectively.

The thought of Sandy being a lesbian bothered him far more than he cared to admit to himself in the autumn of 1969.

Sandy Bloom would not go quietly from his thoughts. She stayed uninvited with him for days after so brusquely welcoming Boaz home to Buffalo, as he nursed his fury toward her for using him. Her leaving town was a gift, because he never had to deal with the situation. He did not see it that way. Whenever she might return, he would have to confront her. But Sandy meant what she said. She never returned while he remained in the city of Buffalo.

What Boaz did not realize was, his days in that city were numbered . . . *and not a high number at that.*

He found himself swimming in a sea of utter distain for women. In retrospect, it displayed a horrible overreaction, the laying of a foundation for a seawall that never needed to be built. But we all live in the present, just like Boaz, where the shoreline appears closer than it is, and we still manage to drown in our good intentions. Over the next few weeks, Boaz dismissed Sandy Bloom from his mind, but not before he made several critical errors.

The simplest and most ruinous of them had to do with women . . . all women. He blamed them all, not just Sandy, for their deception and duplicity. Now that was a mistake for which he would pay dearly. No, not money. Money can be repaid. Turning your back on every female for the imagined offense of one constitutes a bad tactical, if not downright idiotic, move. But do not tell that to Boaz, at least not for the next several years. He was not listening.

You have to give the man a little credit for thinking big. Many of us would balk at the notion of dismissing all women. Not Boaz. While he never considered himself a particularly adept athlete, there he was, jumping to the wrong conclusion with an agility that should have come after years of practice, but did not. Boaz proved to be a natural at taking a simple idea to its simply incorrect, complex conclusion.

Thoughts of Judith began to slip from his memory. He had tried to contact her. She did not speak with him or did not want to speak with him. He assumed she preferred to not be reminded of any implications brought on by their tryst in Hollywood.

At the TV station, events took a turn for the worse. Boaz knew his job, but his irrational fear of being found out betrayed him. Promotion copy for ads or on-the-air announcements came naturally to him. Dealing with the everyday publicity situations of the station where he was the promotion manager held no mysteries for him. He was good, and frankly, that brought a creative tinge to the on-air and printed image of the station. They hired him because he could do just that.

Sandy had left town, and Boaz paid more attention to that fact than his work. To say he became sloppy would be kind. To say he could not find one word to follow another would be more accurate and did lead to more confusion. Boaz messed up again and again without apparent reason to the station executives. Listing his transgressions would not help, neither the station nor Boaz. Boaz had run the traffic light and only awaited the ticket being handed to him for his wrongdoing.

It came at a late September regional meeting of stations owned by UBN in Amarillo, TX. Out of character, Boaz drank too much. Really, the guy who could barely handle two drinks used up all the fingers of one hand counting his vodka martinis.

And just maybe a few more fingers. The fact that Boaz was a quiet drunk helped him not at all. He was noticed by those who could hold their drinks better and could turn him out to face the world without a job. As soon as the regional meeting ended and he returned to Buffalo, Boaz was fired.

October reached the city with all the trees turning red and yellow and brown. It was spectacular the closer you lived to Canada, and the region around Buffalo did not disappoint. The weather turned cold, as it always did, and chilling rains turned to occasional snow a bit earlier that year. Once the snowfall began in earnest, it usually remained on the ground in the cold air until May, the following year. The beauty of this autumn colored everyone's lives in this blue-collar town by the Niagara River where it flows into Lake Erie, except for Boaz.

He missed the winter edging its way down to Buffalo from Canada, because he left for Philadelphia almost immediately after his abrupt departure from the TV station. His father lived in Philly and had offered him sanctuary from the chaos around him. Boaz never returned to Buffalo, though he learned a long time later that Sandy did.

Chapter Six

Boaz Goes to Ground:
Early 1970s

Winter in Philadelphia is not a great deal different than in Buffalo. Perhaps because it is a geographically larger city by almost two-thirds, the snow on the ground casts a dirtier shadow over the narrow streets with their row houses.

Into this pessimistic landscape came a man nursing his imaginary wounds. If you were to ask Boaz what that particular winter season was like, he could not tell you. Largely, feeling sorry for himself clouded his view, mixed in with a generous amount of anger.

Curiously, he did not drink liquor during this time. Much easier than the thoughts of women, Boaz wiped the reason that got him fired off his palette. Perhaps he was not a drunk, anyway. He spent much of that winter cleansing Sandy from his thoughts.

He actually succeeded. Unfortunately, sweeping his brain clear of her meant the few women in his life found themselves swept away as well.

Other than Judith from Atlanta, these other women passed from his thoughts easily. They were all innocent of any crime against Boaz, but *a purge rarely discriminates*. If you are going to condemn all women, you must be thorough about it. "Out with all of them," thought Boaz.

So that is what happened. Over the winter months, he threw them out. Casual acquaintances from Buffalo were tossed out of his mind along with Sandy and Judith. It took great effort and, heaven knows, great quantities of self-pity, but by spring Boaz felt free of women.

Although it appears to be a contradiction because he actually had to think about them during his Philadelphia winter, gone from his thoughts were Eva, the girl he met at a Christmas party; Wanda, the cleaning lady who was too pretty to be a cleaning lady, Boaz thought; and Yolanda, a designer who came to the TV station to be interviewed on one of the programs. Each had allowed themselves to become intimate with the promotion manager of a the TV station. Boaz already knew that even a small bit of fame carried with it some reward.

Honestly, it should be said that Yolanda made him *her conquest*, not the other way 'round. She had appeared one afternoon for a fairly standard interview on the local show called *Buffalo Gals*, hosted by an extremely ambitious lady who Boaz did not like.

The interview session ran late. Cameramen and crew packed up and left immediately afterward so they could run home to explain to their families why they were late for dinner.

There were plenty of workers, including cleaning crew still at the station, but a feeling of emptiness had set in.

Boaz had watched part of the show out of curiosity. Yolanda was well known locally, and her long, blonde hair and form-fitting dress only added to her allure.

She had enough going for her that Boaz watched from the rear of the TV studio without prompting by the cameramen. They proved to be an excellent bellwether for telling you when extra-pretty ladies showed up at the station. But Boaz had accidentally seen her enter the front door about an hour before she was scheduled to be interviewed for the live show. "This gal," he said to himself, "I have to see close up."

Once things quieted down at the station, and the interview finished, Boaz turned to return to his office. Yolanda stopped him.

"Does your office have the two most important items for any station executive?," she asked, in a very quiet voice.

"And what might those two items be?," Boaz retorted.

"A bottle of bourbon and a lock on the door," replied she of the long, blonde hair.

"I have both those things," said Boaz, "and a third item I will show you once those first two has been taken care of. He decided that, if seduction was in the air, *that breeze* would blow in both directions.

To admit that the next hour-and-a-half contained frantic moments filled with heavy breathing and many less-than-human noises might seem a gross understatement, but it did happen. What surprised Boaz most of all? Most of those moments were authored by Yolanda. The lady knew what she wanted and took it. Loudly and ferociously. There was no subtlety. No true feeling. In short, there was no Judith.

Boaz had heard from one of the cameramen that Yolanda was not her real name. He did not care. In Boaz' mind, stating her real name cast a dark cloud over the innocence of whatever label her parents had chosen. Except *Mazie*. Boaz had always hated that name, but he could not tell you why.

The moment passed. Boaz stirred himself out of his revelry and away from these passing thoughts of women he had known. With a grand sweep of his hand, he dismissed all the innocent women who had crossed his path.

He realized he had thrown much of it away. That was fine with him. His return to Philadelphia and to weather that matched his dark mood suited Boaz.

He returned home. When all paths seem closed to us — at one of the nadirs of our life which we hope do not occur too often, we do what Boaz did — we go home.

Not all have such a choice. Geography and relationships determine the circumstances that control whether we even have a home to which we can return. At this low point in his life, Boaz did realize *he could return home*. Jon Gluzzman greeted him.

Harvey L. Brown

William Penn Welcomed Boaz Home

The familiar sight of Billy Penn atop City Hall put the exclamation point behind the dreary day on which Boaz returned to the city where he was born and matured.

His father was a simple man who had always told him, from the time he had matured into an adult, that this was his home and he would always be welcome here. Dad had aged into his late sixties. His mother had died during the early 1960s. The old man had to run the household by himself, and he kept the home immaculate. Boaz became a welcome addition.

Jonathon Gluzzman realized as soon as he saw his son that all was not well. But he came from a generation of European-born parents who had routinely faced adversity and never held back or qualified their love.

His untutored background prevented Jon from completely understanding what his son felt at this moment. It did not matter to him. Boaz needed a place and some space to repair his wounds. His father was simply glad to offer the sanctuary.

Throughout the cold and blustery months that characterized Philadelphia every winter, Jon Gluzzman provided the physical and spiritual warmth Boaz required. Most certainly, he was not the first nor the last parent who, while he knew nothing about medicine, figured out exactly how to help his son heal.

The secret required no degree from a university. Instinctively, Jon let his son alone to recover from his self-inflicted wounds. He helped when asked. He watched when he was not asked. More parents should learn that technique.

His father had worked hard all his life as a salesman. Listening to the customer defined the job in Jon's mind. His life behind the sales counter included the Great Depression of the 1930s, World War II, and the blossoming of America as it finally occupied the West Coast. He sold suits and shirts, socks and suspenders, indeed, all kinds of haberdashery to Philadelphians of all shapes and color.

Throughout his sales career, he worked for only one, quite large haberdashery store. Through good times and bad, Jon Gluzzman never looked elsewhere for work.

Gluzzman's Apparel became a Philly landmark, successful enough to hire some of the first few Blacks as salespersons. No one seemed to mind, especially if they proved to be good at their job. When you think about it, the clerks doing the selling form part of the background, a voice you hear as you examine a piece of clothing. The clientele paid little attention to the person behind the voice.

Despite having his name on the marquee above the main door and everywhere else, too, Jon was not the owner. That distinction belonged to his brother, Herbert. It did account for Jon's staying at the same workplace for over twenty years. Herb paid him well. Besides, he liked his brother. They worked well together.

When Jon married, Herb was always helpful, especially where Boaz was concerned. Herb married also, but his wife was barren. They had no children to occupy their lives. She died in the early 1960s. Herb was left utterly alone.

Jon retired finally in 1957. He took care of Minnie, his beloved wife, until her health failed completely some five years later, and she passed. Boaz had already left home for work in television in New York City and later in Buffalo. His return in the early 1970s both surprised and delighted his father. It kept him alive for the year Boaz spent with him. When Boaz left for the second time, Jon lost interest in life; he died in 1975.

* * *

Sometime in February, 1972, Boaz did have one redeeming thought about Judith. He permitted himself another look at their meeting in Hollywood. Warmth flooded his whole being, along with the realization that today, he had nothing left in his life to offer her.

Had he been able to reconnect with her once he had returned to Buffalo, when he still had his job at the station, he felt it might have changed the direction of his life. Boaz regretted that. It marked the beginning of his coming to grips with what he had done to himself. He saw no solutions. Still, his regret was real. About time.

One of the interesting aspects of hitting rock bottom has to do with direction. There is only one direction left: up! By the spring, Boaz began to think ahead . . . or up. Not very far ahead; it was a new direction for him. To be succinct about his new direction: Boaz realized that the rest of his life lay ahead of him, and he had better begin planning now. He desperately needed four new walls to close around himself. That part he figured out easily. But what new environment? It had to be so different that it would wash away all thoughts of his life until now.

The suggestion came from a woman he had known casually for years. She made costumes for the Community Theater Playhouse, where, many years earlier, he had acted and worked behind the scenes. In this iteration with the playhouse, Boaz helped out in the Box Office, where he showed a discipline that helped with counting money.

Not exactly a job that demanded much from him, except concentration. That proved to be a good focus, though it could be argued that any focus for Boaz provided a step toward a better day.

He had confided his thoughts to a few of the people that he knew from days gone by. They were aware of his misery and his search, and because they were good people, they did not judge him. They did try to help with several suggestions: pick a country in Europe, or go south to Mexico and lose yourself to a new language; go north to Canada where you can be surrounded by several billion trees, not one of whom is a woman.

Colorful, maybe, but Boaz did not connect with any of those places.

There had to be an instant connection. When you think about it, it resembles something like falling in love, though without the stress from seeking and finding a woman. That proved to be just fine with Boaz.

The elderly costume lady blurted it out several times over a period of a few weeks. "San Francisco," she said, "go to San

Francisco. You can start a new life. No one will care about your past. No one will judge what you were, only who you are."

Boaz knew that people have selective hearing; they basically hear only those portions of the conversation they wish to hear. For the first time in his memory, he experienced selective hearing. While it must have occurred previously, Boaz was not aware of it happening to him. The first, second, third times the lady suggested San Francisco, Boaz did not listen nor hear. Oh, he heard her, all right. But selectively wiping out what he did not consider important was a specialty with him. He was good at it. Too good.

Boaz could not tell you at what point he actually heard the woman suggest San Francisco, but one day, he listened, and he heard, and he considered the idea.

Persistency pays off. It did with Boaz. Now that the idea of where to go had penetrated the defenses of his thinking, he saw the instant connection. Striking out on his own in the West held a certain fascination. Walking over the same hills as he had seen often in the movies proved very romantic. Finding his way in the modern world stirred his imagination. Boaz was carried away by these thoughts and his role in their execution.

So he dreamed. He planned. He drew up an itinerary for a two-week experiment that would answer many of his questions. He would travel around the Bay Area for the first week, then look for a job the second week. Boaz was clever enough to understand that he probably would not find a job during that one week. Still, you never know. So he bought airfare tickets and mapped out his hotel reservations and the various places he thought he should see. Finally, Boaz made one resolution: his final decision to move to San Francisco would be held back until he returned from his trip to the West.

For a young man as messed up as he was, he was beginning to exhibit both logic and a commitment to his life. Anyone might look on his awakening as a positive sign, but really, it meant more than that . If this idea panned out, Boaz reasoned there could be a new life for him in this far-away place. The people at the playhouse rejoiced with him.

He thanked them all for believing in him. The costume lady got the biggest hug, because even Boaz could feel that maybe, just maybe, *the rest of his life had begun.*

So he flew to a sunny and mild San Francisco from a cold and wet Philadelphia on a cloudy day in March. Had this been his vacation, it would have shown brilliant planning that left behind, for a fortnight anyway, the winter weather typical of the Northeast.

The six-hour flight proved gruesome to his middle-aged bones. Although he was no stranger to flying, Boaz had traveled non-stop for this long only once before now, and that was to Hollywood, where this adventure began. His body refused to acclimatize itself to the seat nor the recirculated air in the cabin. The effect of this time and space differential was to separate his world into two parts. By getting off the airplane in San Francisco, he entered his new world, a much more open society, and felt a complete separation from the environment in which he grew up.

San Francisco captures beauty unlike most other cities of the world. Its hills effectively change the scenery with each passing block. Many of its structures still capture the quaintness of a by-gone era that began in the 1850s with a Gold Rush. Chinatown and its surrounding neighborhoods display somewhat hidden alleys and narrow streets that, with very little imagination, take you back to a long-lost time. The city charms you in whatever direction you look.

People come there from all over the world to gaze with you. Some stay, some return to where they came from. Each has a story to tell. Even Boaz would share his tale of woe eventually with a trusted friend or two. But that was in the future. True to his word, he toured the Bay Area for the first week and hunted for a job during the second week. He liked what he saw and breathed in the palpable atmosphere. Boaz was hooked.

Although he tried to put off making his decision until he returned to Philadelphia, he knew long before he boarded the airplane flying East that he would return. Boaz spent the next few weeks preparing to drive across the country. The pieces of furniture he had stored with his father would remain in his garage ready for shipment, but not worth the shlep to California. This had to be an economical trip, because Boaz did not have the money for any other kind of trip.

His father, though accommodating, had only his retirement income, and Boaz would never ask him to part with that. So into the rusty old Dodge went mostly clothes and some canned food, several bottles of water and a box or two of crackers. Life on the road could be expensive, and money was scarce at the moment. But he had time and a brain that finally seemed to be working.

Boaz calculated the motel rates pretty accurately, due to the time he spent researching what the trip would cost. He had that money. He had the toll fees and the cost for gasoline over the three thousand miles to San Francisco. When all was ready, he hugged his father and thanked him with all his heart for being there when he was needed. The Gluzzmans were not a kissing family, but they did not love each other less because of that. So a hug and a hand shake would have to do for their parting. Boaz' mother had died about ten years before, or he might have broken the no-kissing rule.

The plan called for a drive of seven days and six nights. True, it could be accomplished faster, but why not see the country. From an airplane you look at clouds and mountains; from the ground you see villages and people, trees and more fields of wheat and corn than Boaz thought possible. The first night was spent in a motel in a forgettable town in Ohio. Nothing about that town was memorable, except the speeding ticket Boaz got for driving faster than a snail through Main Street. He guessed that his out-of-state license plate excited the local cop more than anything else.

Boaz made a ceremony of tearing up the ticket as he crossed the state line into Indiana the following morning. The road ahead really opened up as fields of grain far outnumbered the houses and people. As he relaxed into the routine of driving from sunup to sundown, Boaz found he could add to his mileage each day. Even though he chased the sun by driving west, by sundown he was grateful for a motel with a pool and an early bedtime. He found he could purchase whatever food he needed in the local supermarkets he drove past. A morning coffee always headed the list of required essentials. His outlays for food were minimal.

He stopped every several hours at a state-run roadside rest to nap. He stretched his legs. He watched the people. Like Boaz, they were all going somewhere.

Without pushing himself even close to his limit, he passed through Indianapolis, Des Moines, Lincoln, Cheyenne and Reno, suddenly finding himself crossing into California on the seventh day. A well-planned and well-executed trip. Boaz felt his creative brain cells stirring. San Francisco lay just over the horizon.

* * *

He was home. The City - calling the city *Frisco* was forbidden - became his new home as he worked slowly and with purpose to restore his sense of self worth. When you have a decent job in life, walking with dignity and a feeling of accomplishment incorporates itself into the very way you carry yourself. With that goal in mind, Boaz set himself on his personal road to recovery. He worked for local newspapers and

TV stations, and over the next forty-plus years learned once more to take pride in the abilities he always had.

His life before coming to the Bay Area faded. Except for his relatives, he had no life prior to his walking onto the hills of San Francisco. Gone from his mind was virtually all the hurt experienced in Buffalo, and within a short time, the memory of his visit to Hollywood. The man really knew how to compartmentalize.

Boaz succeeded on all fronts, except one: at the end of more than forty years, he discovered he had aged over forty years. Amazing. How could that have happened? Was he not paying attention? He slowed down in all aspects of his life. He walked more slowly. Running after anything became out of the question. He found that young people on the street regularly passed him walking.

It was his asthma and all his other maladies, Boaz thought. Did he grow up with the asthma, or did it grow up with him? Either way, they had been companions for many years. The diseases and various operations all of us experience throughout our lifetime, capped by the aneurism growing on his aorta brought him closer to old age than his birthdays, according to his doctor.

Still, the idea that disturbed Boaz the most was the young people. He no longer understood many of the things they said or did. They represented a world that had moved on without him.

The jobs he held over those years in The City began with highly-creative work at newspapers and TV stations. After quite a few years, he moved on, working for an insurance company and a restaurant, until he finally settled into managing an apartment building. Such work did not tax his now-limited capabilities. Moreover, he took on various free-lance jobs including writing a column for a magazine. It resembled putting on a glove that fit perfectly.

He enjoyed writing. He found that he could still turn a phrase as well as those young people. Maybe better. Slowly and steadily, Boaz became an old man, but an old man who could express himself on paper.

* * *

One morning, while reading a national newspaper, Boaz came upon a familiar name: Sandra Bloom. Older folks spend far more time reading obituary columns than they probably should, figuring this is where an old friend will achieve their last bit of fame. Now this particular name can hardly be called unusual.

Boaz began reading about this version of the woman with casual interest. She had died a few days prior in a small city in New Mexico, where she had lived for many years with her companion, a woman named Millicent. Sandra Bloom had written several books about the subject that governed her life: the theater. Good for her! And she had been born and lived her early years *in the city of Buffalo, NY.*

Fortunately, Boaz was still brewing his morning coffee, or he would have spilled it in a very unceremonious fashion. Had he stumbled upon an obituary of the person who had changed his whole life? He read on, and not casually at all.

Sandy Bloom — Boaz felt he had better call her by the name he was familiar with — invaded his thoughts as if she had been there for all these years. He felt she was intruding. She always managed to do just that when he knew her. She had been successfully wiped from his memory for so many years that he could not remember when she willingly inhabited his brain.

He wished to remove her immediately. Boaz found that could not be possible until he had satisfied himself that his original estimation of her was correct. He had been convinced years ago she was a lesbian.

Now most obituaries have not reached the point where they blurt out the word lesbian in the announcement. It will come, of course, but for the time being, the closest any official announcement will use openly is denoted by the phrase long-time companion, followed by a woman's name. And there it was. Right in the obituary. Was it proof? Not really. Was it enough for Boaz to convince himself it was proof? *Yes, really.*

"Go back to the oblivion I put you in," Boaz said aloud. Within the minute, maybe the hour, Sandy Bloom disappeared from his conscious thoughts. She returned finally to his subconscious mind, to his bad dreams, where she sometimes lurked on days when his mind wished to chastise him for a new transgression.

Having proved to himself that he had been correct all along about Sandy, Boaz sought to balance his glance backward with what he knew would be a warm memory of Judith. He had known Judith for a few days only; Sandy had been part of his life for a few months. In Boaz' mind, it was never a competition.

Without being aware of it at all, his mind began to admit thoughts he had suppressed for years. Snatches of thoughts of women who he had flung out of his mind began to appear. Without invitation they came, including Judith. Especially Judith.

Chapter Seven

Boaz' Pilgrimage: Atlanta, 2019

Boaz had spent several months and a reasonable amount of money researching Judith's demise some six years previous. The time had come to do something about the sketchy scenario he had put together. Deciding that he had to visit her grave in the Atlanta area required no extra thought. He would go.

Most certainly he owed it to the woman he had forcibly put out of his mind for so long. Asking for her forgiveness once he arrived there was the first step; the second step would be much more difficult, and Boaz had no idea how to accomplish it, or even set it in motion.

He wanted to bring Judith back to life temporarily.

It would be a mistake for anyone to think Boaz was not serious. Boaz was serious about everything these days: his work, his acquaintances, and most of all, repairing the mess he had made of his life. Boaz would be the first one to remind you that he had no idea yet how much he had changed Judith's life and what role he had played in it. He intended to find out.

The most direct way of accomplishing that would be to ask her. Do not underestimate that man. He was mature, now. He knew what he wanted. He knew what he had to do. If that meant speaking with a dead woman, then Boaz would certainly do just that.

If you wish to condemn that old man for proposing the impossible, then you do not deserve to hear the rest of this tale. Because, here is a little look-ahead secret: he actually does what he sets out to do. So leave that man alone.

The planning phase of the trip to Atlanta would require some assistance from Rocky, his long-time friend. You met him earlier when Boaz told you what he said about that fateful month of August, 1969. He referred to the Manson shootings. Rocky always had an interesting perspective on things. Trying to guess what it would be usually proved to be a challenge for a fool. You, not Rocky. Rocky was always sure of the ground he was standing on. You simply had to figure out where that piece of real estate was.

Yes, Rocky was an interesting guy, and over the years, he and Boaz enjoyed each other's company. It amounted to the perfect relationship, because there was no exceptional relationship. Mostly, they traveled together, ate together, went to at least two Major or Minor League Baseball games in every city and town they visited all over the country. Rocky and Boaz booked separate rooms everywhere, and both preferred it that way. Boaz kept a monetary score of what each guy purchased.

At the end of the their sojourn in Phoenix or Seattle or Houston and many other places, one guy might owe the other somewhere in the vicinity of ten bucks. Each trip took three, occasionally four days, and they were back in The City. They accomplished exactly what they set out to do: see baseball games, a different city, along with at least one, often two good meals. They did not have time to be bored.

The trip to Atlanta would follow the same pattern, except Rocky wanted to attend the Women's Final Four Basketball Tournament in New Orleans prior to the Atlanta trip. No matter. Basketball was not Boaz' favorite sport, so he would fly directly to Atlanta. Such variations never annoyed either of them. When they traveled to a new city, they lived well and ate well. And they laughed a lot.

Atlanta would include one Major League game and one Minor League game. Additionally, Rocky promised to take Boaz to the cemetery to pay his respects to Judith. It was not really out of the way, and Rocky, an excellent driver, always rented a car on their trip. With the dates, hotel and places they would visit set, the Atlanta Pilgrimage had been scripted.

Boaz felt exhilarated. At long last, he realized that he might lift the burden he carried with him for over fifty years. True, he had not recognized during that period that all, or even some of the blame lay squarely on himself, but his conscience lost no time in passing that information on to his brain again and again. Knowing that a problem exists puts a person halfway along the path to its solution. If you wish to continue toward the solution, you must begin the hard task of looking for an answer. Boaz felt, with absolute certainty, he was moving toward raising the burden off his shoulders.

He thought about texting Rocky to suggest a jazz club he had noticed during his internet meanderings around the area they would be staying, but the date on the calendar told him that Rocky was probably engrossed in a basketball game in New Orleans about now, so it would have to wait. It might be a better idea to spring it on him later.

Rocky and Boaz engaged in an informal competition where each guy proposed a side trip for an activity or restaurant designed to make this outing a better trip. Rocky had already recommended a restaurant in a distant section of Atlanta. Boaz knew his was the better choice to become the side trip both would eventually agree would become the highlight of the trip. Rocky, you see, liked *jazz* even more than he enjoyed *food*.

There was no need for last-minute packing. Boaz had packed his luggage weeks ago. The man even indulged in a new piece of luggage. It had four wheels instead of the usual two. Boaz had finally come to understand that those smaller, spinning versions moved more easily than the slightly larger version he currently owned and had to pull along behind him. He would be reluctant to admit that the two-wheel suitcase required extra effort for his eighty-four-year-old body, but it did.

His new luggage glided right along. He checked the weather forecast for Atlanta one more time to be certain his choice of clothing matched the temperature in the locale. Satisfied, he hummed a few bars of the theme of that ancient TV show, *Wagon Train*, and off he went to the airport.

You will have to forgive Boaz if he thought that flying to Atlanta on this glorious morning might not require an airplane. But he used one, anyway.

* * *

A layover in Denver constituted the only diversion worth noting about the flight to the Atlanta airport, the busiest one in the U. S. and the end of a long search. It had become late afternoon by the time Boaz made his way north of the city to the hotel where he and Rocky would spend the next three days. They greeted each other, and once the room formalities were over, dinner loomed large on the immediate agenda.

"Not far," begged Boaz. "I've had enough traveling for one day." So they settled on B.B.Q. chicken at a bodega about ten minutes from the hotel. Messy and delicious. What more could you ask for? Boaz enjoyed everything he saw in his short time in Atlanta. Even now, he could actually imagine his feet just touching the ground following the cross-country flight. He knew and understood the mission of this trip, because it translated into the mission of his life as he found himself walking on Atlanta's streets.

The streets of Atlanta were laid out in the mind of a mad, indeed insane, person. Somehow, that person knew to draw straight lines for the downtown area, and as the city expanded, it did so in a kind of circular fashion. Then the craziness set in. Roads do not have to meander, often coming back on themselves 180 degrees. It might have been pleasant if Atlanta contained only a few roads like that. But it does not.

Atlanta has become a maze that challenges all except its native sons and daughters. Perhaps that is what they wanted: to confuse the outsider, the interloper who would disturb the tranquility of this pleasant, Southern city. Other cities throughout the country have streets that wander, seemingly aimlessly, but only Atlanta has called most of them by the same name.

Why are all the streets also labeled with some *Peachtree* connotation? Certainly, it evokes a Southern glow, a built-in reference to the charm, the fragrance, the history of the most prosperous city in the South. *But virtually every street?* Or, so it seems.

Surely, the planners could have referenced a different tree, bush or agricultural product. The people of Atlanta do not lack imagination. A rebuilt city emerged after the Civil War. A few more straight streets, alleys or avenues not named *Peachtree* would have helped.

A charming, old taxi driver once told Boaz that Peachtree Street/Road/Alley and all its other designations in the city of Atlanta and into the surrounding suburban communities are actually the same thoroughfare. When it crosses to another community it becomes a new street with a new name. But Southerners seem to dislike change, so *Peachtree* attaches itself to the new name. Boaz decided he would believe the old man once his brain told him it was a logical explanation. But his brain never did quite agree.

Perhaps it was all a plot to confuse those confounded Yankees should they ever return to destroy Atlanta a second time. You will have ask a native to find out.

Dr. John Pemberton offered Boaz and Rocky a Coke. Dr. John's outstretched arm offers that same opportunity to everyone who approaches the life-sized statute of the creator of the world-famous drink. Boaz and Rocky arrived at Pemberton Place in the morning of the following day to see what Atlanta had to offer.

They chose Atlanta's most well-known location. The normal work day had just begun. A few hours lay before the two adventurers prior to their having to leave for the ballpark.

This brought them to the plaza containing two of Atlanta's most visited sites: the Coca-Cola tour and the the famous Aquarium, on the opposite side of the plaza. Soft drinks or fish. They had time for only one visit before the baseball game. Rocky blurted out his choice of *Georgia Aquarium* before Boaz had a chance to say anything.

"There you go, again," countered Boaz, "speaking out before I get an opportunity to vote on our next adventure."

"What's your choice?," Rocky said in a lowered voice. "I believe in democracies as long as you agree with my opinion."

"You said *Aquarium* before I could say *Aquarium*. Let's go and see if the creatures of the oceans and rivers of the world have come to work today," added Boaz.

With an exaggerated bow toward Dr. John Pemberton from both Rocky and Boaz in unison, the nineteenth-century biochemist was left holding his empty glass of Coke.

Across the plaza, some ten million gallons of water awaited, separated neatly into exhibits for the many different mammals, invertebrates and, wouldn't you know, fish of all shapes and sizes. Natural habitats emerged from the cave-like interiors. The penguins waddled around outside the water. Rocky and Boaz watched as they dove under the surface.

In all the exhibits, the thick plexiglass separating human from beast permitted a look at their life below the surface. With the huge king crabs, for example, life below the water- line took up almost all their existence. Most exhibits held species that could live together, with plants and other underwater vegetation they knew from their original part of the world. Only the piranhas seemed not to share their habitat.

"I don't want them living in my neighborhood," opined Rocky. "Too many teeth," he added. "Many of my neighbors are too old to have any teeth."

"Invite them over for lunch. Unfortunately, lunch will be you," suggested Boaz. "Just look at how placid they seem. Must not be feeding time, yet.

Having exhausted their meager supply of piranha jokes, Rocky and Boaz plowed on through the shark exhibits, the seals, and always, the exotically colored fish from the world's oceans and seas. It constituted a world so different from theirs. Beautiful and vibrant, the occupants of the world's waters are living very nicely in a microcosm of their native setting at the Georgia Aquarium.

"I'm in love," interrupted Boaz, as they reached the white Beluga whales exhibit. "Have you seen such a soft, curvy animal that really deserves to be hugged?" Sure enough, the large, docile creatures swam pressed against their invisible boundary as if they too, wanted to be hugged. Boaz was smitten.

Rocky countered with "Look at this guy. He travels completely across the country to meet with a dead woman, and before he can even accomplish his mission, he's making eyes at another woman. It says on the sign that *female* Belugas are smaller."

He had to physically pull Boaz away from the beautiful Belugas and on to the scheduled trained dolphin show about to begin. There, they watched the cleverest of sea creatures prove how much better they are at contortion than us. The dolphins had such rapport with their trainers that you began to wonder *who was taking who* for a swim.

Rocky and Boaz left the Aquarium slightly dazed, but filled with wonder for a world they knew so little about. Dr. John Pemberton did not seem to mind being ignored. As they passed him on the way to the ballpark, the statue even offered them a drink again.

The way to the ballpark would have been charted by Rocky before he arrived in Atlanta. He knew his job and never failed to get them to the game on time. Boaz had to make certain

Rocky got to enjoy what he had driven thousands of miles for: a Braves day game this afternoon, and a trip to Rome, Georgia tomorrow for a Minor League baseball game that evening. Before that excursion, they would enjoy a grand, well-planned lunch, and then visit the cemetery. He did not mind waiting an extra day in Atlanta to visit Judith at the cemetery.

Boaz had not figured out yet how to bring back this woman from the dead, but he was working on it. The interruption of a baseball game only served to whet his appetite. He was close to solving his dilemma. He could feel it. Boaz spent most of the ballgame they watched that afternoon far away, lost in his thoughts. The dull game that day helped him remain in his own world.

In the last day leading up to his departure to Atlanta, where he would meet up with Rocky, Boaz received the surprise of his life: an answer to his repeated inquiries about Esty through a text. She briefly and a bit formally acknowledged that her aunt was indeed buried where Boaz thought she was, and agreed to show him the exact place in the cemetery.

Within seconds, a reply went out inviting Esty and Max Odesa to lunch at a very nice restaurant where the Chattahoochee river slowed itself down by bending and twisting to create a few new beaches and then pass on.

You could not find a more idyllic setting for a luncheon. Boaz had never been to Atlanta. His knowledge of this restaurant stemmed from a decent amount of research into eateries not far from the hotel where Rocky and he were staying. It was not magic that Boaz knew about the restaurant, or that they accepted; the magic would come later when he brought Judith back so they could speak to each other.

At the appointed time, at the place noted, Boaz and Rocky met Esty and Max. The formal introductions had taken place some twenty minutes ago. Rocky then politely, but quickly, made off for the bar on a level slightly below and to the right of their table. Boaz wasted no time filling his guests in on Rocky's quirkiness and their relationship. Rocky steadfastly kept his word, once made, but he already had heard Judith's story a few times. As all three watched, Rocky settled himself between two very beautiful Southern belles and was happily chatting them up.

"I already owe Atlanta a debt of thanks," began Boaz to Esty and Max, "for crossing off one of those important questions on my Personal Bucket List. Shortly before Rocky and I planned this trip in detail, I became very sick for about three-and-a-half weeks. As I lay in bed unable to drink much of anything, I opted for Coca-Cola instead of coffee in the morning. It worked. I had always wondered why Southerners drank Coca-Cola instead of coffee to start their day. Yeah, it works. I do not know why, but it does."

Boaz looked straight at Esty, and continued, "It was your mother, I'll bet, who gave you the green light to meet with the man who knew your aunt."

"That's true," Esty replied. "My mother believes that any request to a Southern Lady by a gentleman that is simple, sincere and ever-so-slightly sexy should be complied with."

"But I was not . . ."

Esty interrupted. "My mother sees sex everywhere. She likes life a little salty. Aunt Judith did everything by the book. She blasted the way so we might all follow. There is almost no one in this world I revere more. So, if your plans include anything . . . *anything* that throws dirt at my Aunt Judith, stop here."

"Absolutely not," answered Boaz. "It took me just over fifty years for me to realize how much in love with your aunt I am. I can only apologize for my lapse. I will not apologize for my love."

How is it possible for the great waiters and waitresses to know exactly when to serve the luncheon? In Atlanta, they do it with pomp and ceremony. Table chatter ceased quite suddenly as the procession of servers and musicians approached their table. The roving string players appeared, the seafood, hot and steaming, followed, wine glasses were refilled, and Boaz never got to say another word. At least not for the next forty minutes. Even if you were to ask him, Boaz would never admit he arranged it all.

Dessert was finished. With grace and considerable charm toward his two luncheon companions, Boaz stood up to get the waiter's attention. With one hand he signaled the time had come to pay. With the other, the ever-attentive Rocky picked up his signal to abandon plans to take Atlanta by storm. General William Tecumseh Sherman of the Union army might not have approved, but Boaz did.

This procession had a date with a dead woman. So they marched, Esty and Max leading the way, Boaz and Rocky following. As they exited the Grand Patio, Boaz looked around informally to determine if he could notice anyone else that Esty and Max might have brought along to evaluate the Western interlopers. He could see none. In fact, there were none. Esty had her standards, also.

True, they were more than a half-hour later than they said they would be, yet no one dared complain. Not even Judith, who had the right without the voice. Had anyone, aside from Boaz, ever asked her what she felt? We dismiss our dead. Once gone, the harshness of the edge defining life and death hones us into overlooking what the dead would have wanted.

The visit to the grave was pleasant and efficient. Perhaps too much so. Boaz resolved in his own mind he would not be able on this day to reach Judith. He determined to return to Judith's gravesite by himself the next morning. Bringing Judith back to life was Boaz' problem. No one else could or should be asked to participate.

Situated not far from a paved road, the grave itself offered no clue to Boaz how to achieve his monumental task. Yet he was overcome by the closeness he felt by being so near to the person he had sought from a distance of many miles and a lifetime of misadventures. He returned to the promise he had made to himself as he began his search to find Judith.

"We shall be together sometime, I swear," Boaz had said.

But the proximity to her grave did not fit that definition. He wanted more. He wanted to enter her soul. Boaz saw the two of them as spirits, as souls entwined forever.

Standing next to her grave lacked the complete fulfillment he was seeking. But, for the time being, it would have to suffice.

Esty and Max stood a short way away to give Boaz a small, private space. Rocky decided to remain in the parking lot to clean the car's windshield for the long trip ahead.

Boaz looked down at the grave of a woman who had traded ideas with him that made both of them smile. They had bonded. They had made love. They had reached into each other's depths looking for their souls. And Boaz began to feel Judith's soul struggling to reach him. That feeling remained only for an instant, then vanished.

Boaz said what he had traveled thousands of miles to say. "I'm sorry. I forgot you, and I will never forget you again . . . nor your incredible smile. I came not just because I wanted to, but because I had to. Know one thing: I have rediscovered how much I love you. That is what I came to say. Whatever else I might say would only distract from that simple and completely true fact." Boaz ended with, "Forgive me."

With that, they all left the gravesite.

After a pleasant leave-taking, Boaz and Rocky settled in for the sixty-mile drive to Rome, GA, north and a little west of Atlanta. It was the last part of their pact when planning the pilgrimage. Rome, GA was founded in 1834. It displaced the Cherokee village on that site when the tribe, along with many other Native-American tribes were pushed west to Oklahoma on what became known as the Trail of Tears.

The White plantation owners of Georgia filled that void with Catholic immigrants from Italy. It proved to be a convenient repository for newcomers that the kingmakers did not want populating the area to the south, especially around Atlanta. They gave it the name Rome for obvious reasons, and Rome, many years later, gave Boaz and Rocky a chance to see a Minor League game.

A game was scheduled for that evening. Seeing the single-A class Rome Braves usually meant baseball played by young kids still learning the game professionally. They played with the enthusiasm of the teenagers they were, mostly. It was fun to watch. It always renewed their old-timers' faith in the game of baseball.

"Let's sit on the opposition's side of the field," offered Rocky. "I'm not sure how long either of us would survive with you in that Phillies cap." Because they always bought tickets to local settings like this one after they arrived, it proved no problem. Rocky and Boaz loved the between-innings little races by very young kids, the local beer, and the fireworks that highlighted special games.

Sometime about the fifth inning, Rocky began his somewhat strange ritual. He left the seats they bought and disappeared for the next couple of innings. Many baseball games ago, Boaz learned Rocky liked to walk the entire perimeter of the park, stopping to view the game from a different angle. It was Rocky being Rocky. After the game, the long drive back to the Atlanta hotel proved no problem for this most efficient and safe driver.

Boaz slept well that night. When he woke up, he still had the same problem he could not solve yesterday. Where was Judith? So this morning, he called Rocky and told him to go to the CNN news and Fox theater tours and exhibits alone. Rocky would not need a second invitation; he looked forward to that experience.

That was one of the things Boaz liked about Rocky: when their interests diverged — when they took a different path, they could briefly go their own ways while still traveling together. It enhanced each guy's personal trip and did not interfere with the overall enjoyment they had when together. In fact, it enlivened each person's appreciation of the trip as they traveled together to cities and towns around the country. While it had been pleasant enough finding and seeing the gravesite with Judith's niece and nephew, as well as Boaz' accommodating traveling companion, he felt that he could not connect with Judith's spirit with all those people crowding the space around the grave. Not that they were not nice about his initial visit. They accommodated his wishes perfectly and left him alone with Judith for about ten minutes.

But Boaz felt he just did not connect with Judith. Too many people, he guessed. It was not their fault; they were all especially considerate of his desire to speak directly to the spirit of the woman he had traveled so far to be with.

It became crystal-clear to Boaz that the only way he would ever bring Judith back to life would be if he visited with her alone.

A cynical Rocky would have sensed that Boaz simply wished to be by himself so that he might invent any story he chose to. After all, is that not what old men and women do when confronted with an impossible reality? Boaz could not, nor would not, speak for other old people. He was sincere in his quest for a conversation with the spirit of a dead woman and did not care whether anyone thought he fantasized.

"Old age," Boaz concluded, "sets you free to travel to travel to places others dare only dream about. And that is where I will find Judith."

Chapter Eight

Boaz Meets Judith:

Atlanta, 2019

The next morning, it was only a short taxi ride of about three miles from the hotel to Eternal Gardens. He directed the driver down a path that ran close to the gravesite. They would have gone a bit further, but the taxi driver showed unusual uneasiness at driving in a cemetery. The taxi stopped abruptly. Boaz paid the fare and continued on alone. The taxi, he noted, made a U-turn and exited the park at a rate slightly faster than it had entered.

Boaz suspected that was not a unusual reaction. People do not enjoy being in a cemetery. "I don't know why," thought Boaz. He could not think of even one instance where a visitor to the graves was disturbed or robbed by the inhabitants of the park. He long-ago decided that the average person feels they have entered a different world, one that they will eventually be added to, and one that reminds them too strongly, too vividly that here, or a place similar to it, is where they will spend their own eternity.

"Too bad," Boaz said aloud, as he reached Judith's gravesite. "Not one of these residents will borrow something from me and not return it. They won't complain about anything that might disturb them. They won't park in your driveway, nor peer furtively at you through their window when you return home one night a bit worse for wear. On the other hand, you will have to give up the free cookies they might bring over prior to a holiday. The residents of Eternal Gardens will not baby-sit your kids," he said, assuming Boaz had children, which he did not.

He could not help himself; he said "Good Morning" to Judith, and even walked a few steps to a nearby grave to offer the same salutation to the grave of some guy named William. Boaz felt good. The day had started well for him. Most of all, he could now concentrate on a conversation with the spirit of Judith.

The sun had already dried the morning dew covering the grass, and its warmth allowed him to stretch out on the spring grass next to the grave. As Boaz lay on the cool, green carpet, above him a falcon circled, changing direction several times before picking an oversized rock to perch on, just far enough away that he was not too concerned.

Perhaps the bird of prey was just curious. Maybe he considered the stretched-out figure to be lunch. But Boaz finally decided the falcon simply wanted to establish that this was his property, and he just tolerated my presence.

Two groundskeepers came along the path near the grave. One of them pushed a wheelbarrow containing grass seed and a shovel; the other, older fellow carried a rake. They sought out small patches where the grass decided not to grow and filled them in with seed. As Boaz came into their view, they stopped and suggested, politely, of course, that he should be standing on the carefully manicured lawn, not lying on it.

Surprised, Boaz jumped to his feet, realizing almost immediately that the two workers meant no harm to him. He apologized for disturbing their landscape. Still, he could not help asking them a question that had formed in the back of his mind.

"Are you aware of the male falcon flying around this Park," he inquired. "Is it dangerous?" Boaz had read up on falcons last night at the hotel.

"Not onless y'all is a bird or a duck, or maybe a rodent, if they is hungry enuf," replied the older man. "Y'all is talkin' 'bout Scarlett or it could be Rhett. They live in the trees here. Peregrine falcons they is. Married, y'all might say. Falcons stick with the same bird for life. The folks who run this-here park gave 'em their names. Right outta that book, 'Gone With . . . sumtin'. That Scarlett, she's bigger and nicer lookin' 'en Rhett, but that-there Rhett, he ain't afraid of nuttin'."

Boaz concealed how impressed and more than a bit scared he felt about the falcons whose territory he had entered. He watched the two groundskeepers trundle off behind the heavy wheelbarrow until they turned a corner and could be seen no more. It amused him that the people who operated the Eternal Gardens would choose these names from Margaret Mitchell's famous story of the antebellum South for the mated falcons living in their cemetery. However, it did not surprise him. Boaz theorized that more than one pair of falcons in the Atlanta area bore these same names.

He looked up. He caught what he thought was a large bird on the wing with stripes on her chest. The stripes meant she was the female. "I'll bet Scarlett is looking to feed her brood." She quickly disappeared behind some trees. "Watch out, little birds," Boaz cautioned. "You're no match for that that gal." The month of May would come to a close in about a week, so the falcon chicks, known as an eyass, would be clamoring for food from their attentive parents.

Try seeing the cemetery from the falcon's viewpoint: no obstructing houses, almost no concrete pavement, only a few overhead wires to be navigated. On such an expansive estate as this cemetery, filled with trees, vegetation and ponds, a meal could be had easily. For the falcon, it was like going to a deli.

The sun had reached its full height. Noon must have arrived. Boaz stood on the warm grass. Around him the landscaped bushes and straight trees formed a contrived wall closing off the sections. Narrow paths forced visitors in the directions they were meant to travel. Small, tranquil lakes erupted in their center, shooting water high from a spout close to the surface and arching before crashing down again. In the distance, lines of cars filled with a multitude of well-dressed mourners had begun to arrive. Aside from a crypt here and there, built into the side of the sloping land, you would not know this was a cemetery.

Tombstones were nonexistent, replaced by small plaques in the ground. The few buildings that there were contained row-upon-row of above-ground crypts, indicating marshy ground. An auditorium that could seat about 150 people became a very busy place around the middle of the day as multiple funerals slipped in and out of those padded chairs. From an office close by, the staff oversaw the movement of friends and relatives paying their last respects to the recently departed.

Above them all, the falcon had retired to the safety of the tree branches to allow those scurrying below the chance to bury their dead.

PHOTO CREDIT. Guy Bianco via

Beautiful Free Images & Pictures | Unsplash

Boaz looked down at the small metal plaque seemingly pasted where the head of the casket lay and marveled at how little each grave disturbed the surroundings. The nameplate only added about an inch to the height of the manicured grass. You have a name, but we prefer it should not disturb the calculated beauty of the Eternal Gardens. He sat next to Judith's grave, so they could have a conversation.

Boaz had spent most of the long day at Judith's grave, sustaining himself with a small bottle of water and several wrapped fruit bars. He was careful to place the used, empty wrappers in his pocket for later disposal. It was an instinctive reaction. He hated the debris left by others and saw no reason to add to the forgotten waste in the graveyard. Not only were the surroundings beautiful, they commanded his attention and his admiration. He might spoil them with a wrapper or bottle and did not want that to happen. Boaz relaxed and stretched out, again.

"Hi-ya, Boaz"

"What? Who said that? "

"I did. It's Judith. You're lying almost on my grave. Don't you think that's a little bit personal? How would you feel if I lay down next to your grave?"

Without thinking, he answered, "I wouldn't mind at all. You can . . . wait a minute, who are you? Where are you?"

Boaz sat straight up. As far as he could tell, there was no one in sight. He looked instinctively at the grave near him, but nothing there had changed. With some apprehension, he swung his gaze in every direction. Not one person disturbed his line of sight. So who was speaking to him?

"I already told you: I'm Judith. You're here to visit with me. So let's visit. But don't look for me. I'm a voice inside your head."

"But that's absurd. I don't hear voices. I'm not crazy. You can't be real. I refuse to believe what you're saying."

"Think what you want, my dear. True, I'm not real; I'm a spirit. You brought me back to life. I suppose I should thank you for that. On the other hand, there are so many things I don't want to thank you for. Like forgetting about me for more than fifty years. Was that nice? That really sharp guy half a century ago wouldn't do that. I really liked you."

He stood up and backed away from the grave. But that voice inside his head did not need him to be near the grave when she spoke.

"Stop moving, Boaz. I'm not going to hurt you. I may cause you a little discomfort, but you deserve that, in my opinion. You never called me after we got on so well in Hollywood. I deserved better treatment from someone I really liked. Who knows, we could have easily fallen in love. Marriage. Family. A life together. How could I love someone who wasn't there for me to fall in love with?"

Boaz reflected on that assertion. He knew she was right. When they had parted in Hollywood, Judith had filled his mind. He had tried to phone her a few times, but never got through to her. Very soon thereafter, she was gone from his thoughts.

But Boaz persisted, "You are pretty much describing me right now, standing here. And the funny thing is, you're right. You are nowhere, Judith, except inside my head, and I'm finally starting to realize how much my love for you has brought me on this trip to your grave. I think I knew that all along. Now that I have brought you back to life, there is no reason to not tell the truth about how we feel toward each other. Do you agree?"

Curiously, Boaz got no answer from Judith, at least not right away. He paced. From the grave to the nearby paved path and back again, twice. Her spirit was playing hard to get. It occurred to Boaz that he had begun to argue with a voice inside his head. "How strange," he thought.

"I'm here," he said, finally.

"Stop pacing. I know you're here."

"That's not what I mean. I'm here. I came a long way to visit your grave. All the way across the country. From San Francisco. That is further than Huck Finn and Jim, the runaway slave, had floated down the Mississippi river. I came as soon as I could. Once I realized that I had neglected you for fifty years, I came to visit you. I had to. That should mean something to you.

"I have to be honest with you. We have to tell the truth to each other. Otherwise, what we thought we had all those years ago becomes meaningless."

Now Judith had something to say. That voice inside his head got a tiny bit louder. And it spoke with authority.

"The truth," Judith asked? "I wonder how much of the truth any of us know. You're right, you know, to come to me seeking the truth. The problem for both of us is, I don't know the truth, either. You could have gone to bed with a thousand women, and I wouldn't know unless you told me.

"Did you?" Perhaps Judith thought she would catch him off guard. She did not.

Boaz answered with an alacrity that only truth can bring: "No, not a thousand. A few. As I recovered my purpose in life while living in San Fran, my appetite for women returned. It was pleasant, but it never compared to the connection we had."

Not at all put off by Judith's cleverness, Boaz reminded her that he came from a family of honest men. She knew that from their time together in Hollywood; he had made it a point to tell her. So he repeated it for emphasis.

"That's not what I heard," the voice inside his head retorted. "I heard directly from the Black lady's daughter. Your uncle crossed the line with an employee in the early 1960s. I met the daughter shortly before I died. She's all grown now, with a family of her own. A nice woman. She was very troubled by not being able to find her father. I wonder if she ever found your uncle."

Judith, Boaz realized, had stumbled upon an old Gluzzman family secret. Boaz chuckled, confusing Judith, but only slightly.

"I've known about it since shortly after it happened. Sorry for laughing. Actually, it's a big load off my mind. Been wanting to tell about my uncle's *extracurricular activity* for many years now. Uncle Herb told my father, and Dad told me. In those days, my aunt was still living. We kept quiet. Dad and I felt it was the right thing to do. She should not have to pay for the sins of my uncle.

"Funny thing is, Uncle Herb loved both women. My aunt couldn't have children. Uncle Herb loved her without feeling sorry for her, from what I and Dad could see. Never met the Black woman formally, though I knew which employee she was. The way Uncle Herb spoke about her showed a real affection on his part. Still, she left town right after the baby was born.

"Those were the times," concluded Boaz. "If you want to hate me for respecting my family's wishes, I plead *no contest*."

"Boaz, you definitely sound like that bold young man I met in Hollywood. So let us be completely honest. Can you keep a secret? I always loved you . . . "

Boaz interrupted with a thought that had been hiding in his brain. Huckleberry Finn had always stretched the truth. It reminded him of what his creator, Mark Twain, had supposedly said: "Two people can keep a secret, if one of them is dead," which Boaz repeated out loud.

"Really? And which one are you?" Obviously, Judith had no intension of letting him be the joke-teller.

"Very funny, Judith. You do realize, I hope, that because you're dead and I'm not, we are the only ones who can legitimately tell Mark Twain's joke. You might want to tell him that the next time you meet." Boaz' quickness of thought had finally returned.

Boaz was not certain, but he thought Judith was stifling a small laugh. He decided this was as good a time as any to share his thoughts, thoughts he had been saving for himself. He knew that he could only share them with Judith. He had rehearsed his secret during the long airplane flight to Atlanta. Before she might get her secret out, he decided to tell her his. He began in earnest.

"But I may get the last laugh, Judith. One of the reasons I'm here is because my doctor - one of too many doctors - thinks the aneurysm on my aorta is too large, and they think I should have it taken care of. It means going under the knife, and I'm not sure I should. Eighty-four years is a long time to be around. Maybe it's time."

"Whoa, Mr. Know-It-All, are you talking suicide? Let's get something straight: this is my territory you are invading. I do not want your blood spilled on me. Not on my grave, fella. That's a sin."

Boaz could not help but respond, "Against who?"

"Well, against yourself, against me. Why would you even think of such a thing? Do you want to kill yourself after bringing me back to life? You managed to mess up your life and my life, and now you think everything will be better if you come to my grave and lie down on the grass that they mowed only two days ago . . . *to die*."

"It's not suicide. I could go at any second. Coming here means I want to ask your opinion. If I get too excited, then there might be a fatal reaction. I don't know. After more than half-a-century, it's time I did come to you and find out what you think."

That gave Judith a reason to pause and reflect. She answered, "I detect a spark of common sense lighting up your brain. Well, you could be right. People do not die in a cemetery. They are past that point. Some of us are, anyway."

She continued, "If you feel it will prolong your life, have that heart operation. Cling with both hands to the few years of life you have. From my vantage point beyond life, I can say with authority those years are worth having, worth experiencing. Whenever we shall be together for all eternity will come soon enough. You need not hasten it."

Boaz stood and walked a few steps away from Judith. He needed to think. He realized it was not a physical condition his head responded to, but a mental one. Explaining to her all about the up-to-then successful attempts to keep his body intact and functioning would take longer than it might with others. He returned and reviewed for Judith the asthma and hay fever that dominated his whole approach to his existence; his many operations encountered during life, the open-heart surgery that is probably tied into the aneurysm currently growing larger in his aorta, and the very high blood pressure that he experienced because of it. Even the doctors conceded it was dangerous.

They had done a masterful job of probing, patching and circumventing disease and disability. He knew the doctors had done their best, so why was he not more grateful? Instinctively, Boaz knew the answer.

When you understand that your gaze forward in life covers a much shorter distance than your gaze to the rear, and people drop out of your life faster than you can add them - or even want to add them, you must ask yourself why. Maybe a hundred years ago he would have died twenty or more years before now. That made up the natural order of life for centuries. But those medical researchers have pushed forward the time we spend on Earth. We remain beyond the years when our lives would have ended. Even several years ago, our time would have expired simply because no one knew how to save us from natural perils.

Who will bring back loved ones that are gone without being forgotten? Medical research drove up in their ambulance too late to save them. As Boaz looked around, both physically and spiritually he could only see himself. In his small portion of the world, he appeared to be the only survivor.

"Someone like you can bring back love that has been missed, Judith. We never developed that moment we found in Hollywood. It was my fault. I know that. Still, the fact is, I have survived and you have not. And I have been questioning for some time now why I grow old alone. Sure, friends and family will always be there for you. I cherish that. But where are you? How many of us are lucky enough to face the final phase of our existence together with the one we chose long ago. So I miss you."

"You are growing on me, Boaz. As long as we are being honest, you began to grow on me when we first met. During my late twenties, I knew a few men. Well, most of them I have always described as boys, but not one of them could equal you. And you showed guts, Boaz. You kissed me in front of everybody. That meant something to me. I wasn't angry. I liked it a lot. It began for me then."

"If I say it was your fault that I kissed you, it's not because I'm blaming you, Judith. I remember even now you smiling at me. You looked beautiful that night, and I would have told you so right then. But you smiled in that special way you have. I had no defense against that lovely smile. So I kissed you. Who clapped? One person. It should have been everyone in the world."

"One guy had the guts to applaud you, Boaz. Don't make light of him. Maybe he thought it was funny to clap, but you should thank him. It meant that now there were two people who thought you did the right thing. He and I. And you, do you agree? Do you think kissing me was the right thing to do at that moment? You seemed to. If I recall, you got your reward that evening."

"Never looked at it that way. But you're right," he answered. "What an experience. That kiss changed me. As much as I liked you up till then, that kiss and our time in bed sealed my fate. Well, it should have. It didn't.

I returned to Buffalo and immediately became engulfed in such a hateful situation that I blocked out what happened. It came to a head right after we parted in Hollywood. I never realized that you somehow were caught up in my rejection. A kind of guilt-by- proximity. You were gone from my mind. The people who gave me such grief in Buffalo were rejected and put out of my head. Although I tried to contact you, I am sorry, that also included you."

He hunched over, but was careful to look around. No one was in sight. The deep sadness that had been with him since the day long ago when he found her picture after fifty years overwhelmed him. Tears formed, and Boaz made no effort to stop them.

"Now I believe you," Judith said emphatically. "Tears don't lie, my sweet. At least, your tears do not. You have convinced me. We should have been together. We will be together. Someday, when time does not count, when eternity is now. It will come soon enough. Do not hasten the end of your time on Earth. Eternity remains without length and always will be without beginning or end.

"Enjoy your life." she continued. "Life is a beautiful experience. It is filled with a child's laughter, the nuzzle of a pet's nose, the warm hug of another person. They're yours to feel, to enjoy, Boaz. I cannot and will not take them from you. They are beyond me forever. I did enjoy all that. Especially the children. You cannot imagine my joy when the little ones found a piece of chocolate where I had hidden it from them. Or the carrot devoured by a goat. My family and my friends were loved by me, even when I did not bring them a treat," she added, as she valiantly defended her treatment of those closest to her.

Even in death, Judith could not hide the pecking order of her view towards those she loved: foremost were the children, then the animals, and finally, the adults. And here was Boaz, finally making his way into that last category.

Judith began to understand both what life might have been like *with* Boaz, and what life had been like *without* him. That old man poured out his love to her at a point where she could do nothing about it. Life had, indeed, passed her by. She regretted nothing about the way she had lived her life, but, by adding Boaz to the mix, Judith saw that it could have been fuller, more interesting, and it would have contained what what she missed the most: children of her own.

Even in death, Judith harbored no deep-seated dislike for the men who passed through her life. Still, she knew the spark of love was missing. The one time she felt that feeling happened over a few days in Hollywood. It had been snuffed out almost as quickly as it had been discovered. Life - all in the past now - moved on.

Boaz' tears made her wonder. Would he have been a great husband? A wonderful father? From her vantage point beyond life, Judith concluded he would have measured up to her expectations. The problem was, of course, such a conclusion brought on immediate regret.

What if she had tried just a bit harder to find him. Had she or Boaz made contact many years ago, where would that have taken them? Even for a regretful spirit, these proved to be unanswerable questions. But she agreed, *she should have tried.*

Love brings two people together. We all know that is not enough. To create the glue that will bind them together for a lifetime - even beyond a lifetime - both must work at their relationship constantly. Judith thought back to that time in her life when she had reached old age. When her thoughts returned once more to the creative process she so enjoyed when she worked in television.

Never mind the surrounding circumstances. Just being able to make your mind accomplish creative gymnastics brought life back to its sweetest moment. Judith loved that. Could Boaz have helped her? He believed so. And Judith had to agree.

Perhaps Boaz had it right to want to expand those goat stories. Certainly, it was an intriguing suggestion. Judith allowed herself a few seconds in her mind to play with the idea. She recalled how much she enjoyed conjuring up what that goat might have done during the time she actually wrote those stories.

A goat that talked about politics? If Judith's mouth could still water, it would have at that very moment. And the question that invaded her mind was: *why didn't I think of that?*

She did not; Boaz did.

At the gravesite, Boaz fidgeted. He walked around the grave, not once but twice, stuffed his hands into his pockets, took them out, wiped his face with the tissues he used instead of a handkerchief, because he thought handkerchiefs were simply unsanitary. Clearly, Boaz showed that he had something on his mind. For a man who had said only a few minutes prior to this that they *had to tell each other the truth,* he showed that he was having trouble getting something off his chest.

Judith, satisfied that she had removed all thoughts of suicide from his mind, asked Boaz a very obvious question.

"You are upsetting me, Boaz. Not only because you are moving around like a bird who has fallen from its nest, which is bad enough, but if you are in discomfort, then I am, too. I share all your feelings now," Judith noted. "If I am going to be part of whatever bothers you, then at least tell me why I should be upset."

Boaz sat cross-legged next to the grave and blurted out what was really, really bothering him. To tell the truth, it was not what Judith expected.

"When you came back into my life exactly fifty years after we first met, I became obsessed with finding out as much as I could about you. The internet helped a bit. Search machines, which I really did not know how to use - and still don't - told me you had died. That devastated me. On the one hand, the thought of you dying destroyed me, because I thought you were lost to me forever. I did not let that stop me, however. Finding out more about you became my task in life," explained Boaz.

"And would you be so kind as to tell me, what in the name of all that is sacred is bothering you," asked an increasingly impatient voice inside his head.

"You never married," Boaz replied, putting into three words the thought that nagged at his brain since he discovered that fact. "Tell me why. Am I the reason for that?"

To her everlasting credit, Judith did not react. That is because she realized exactly what it was: a simple and completely honest declaration of love. Boaz had become very precious to her. He appeared so vulnerable at the moment that Judith did not want to hurt him. So she lied.

"It's a bit complicated," she replied to the question that came from his heart, "but you deserve to know how I dealt with your disappearance from my life. There was a short pause of several seconds as Judith processed what she might say to breathe life and give form to her lie.

At last, Judith continued, "We were more than just lovers, I felt, when that airplane left California and returned me to reality. I have never felt so comfortable with any man as I did with you. That is true even now. What was missing then was time . . . time to become more familiar with you, to understand you, and to confirm to myself that I was in love with you. It did not happen."

Boaz noted that he had called her several times and never had gotten through to her. Rather quickly, he lost his job in Buffalo, and he felt he no longer had anything like a future to offer her, so he stopped calling. He had concluded, incorrectly, that Judith did not want to remember her affair in Hollywood . . . or Boaz.

"I also lost my job a few years later," added Judith. " I truly could have used your shoulder to lean against then. But I threw myself into my new work as an event planner. You were gone from my life, and I had no time for other men. Every time I thought about being with a man, they paled in comparison to that man in Hollywood."

What Judith had just offered as an explanation provided a truth that approached being 85% correct. Do not push it any further. Even in death, Judith could not bring herself to intentionally hurt anyone, especially not Boaz. In reality, she had one or two proposals, but her complete distaste for Southern men based on her days working in Atlanta television never brought her close to marriage. On that most important subject, Boaz was the clear winner.

As to having a short fling, Judith proved that she possessed an appetite for the opposite sex. Largely in her early years as an event planner, the job sometimes offered an opportunity for indulging in a *quickie*. They rarely lasted more than a one-afternoon stand. Judith enjoyed her freedom to pick with whom she would solidify a deal.

They needed her far more than she needed the extra-curricular activity. Judith knew that and used it to her advantage. Her connection to any of them began and ended with the event she was planning for them.

She was scrupulous to the point of being a fanatic about safe sex and never bent those rules even once. And Judith did not kiss and tell. She was not built that way. Although, on one or two occasions, it proved to be a convenient threat to end the unwanted intentions of an overly-amorous client.

As the early years quickly passed, Judith's appetite for sex diminished. Actually, she became quite bored with it. These men had little to no imagination. A Southerner who could challenge her mind as well as her body proved to be in very short supply among the men Judith knew in Atlanta. Judith could only remember one real man like that.

She suspected that Laura, her assistant during those early years, became really adept at winning jobs for their small company. Judith was not jealous, but cautioned the young and beautiful woman many times about the strict rules of such entanglements.

In only one instance did Judith go to bed with a woman. Chalk it up to curiosity, not compulsion. Never afraid to try a different path, Judith freely admitted to herself —no one else, mind you, that this adventure represented a road in a different direction. It seemed worth exploring, so explore it she did. While it seemed safer, that one night with a woman brought her nowhere near the satisfaction that sleeping with a man gave her. She never repeated the experiment.

Yes, Judith liked men. And she had to admit to herself at last — at long last, that no one connected with her like Boaz did years ago. Funny, she took that thought about Boaz to the grave with her, but it never left her soul.

He turned out to be what he always had been, *her one true love.*

She forgave him completely because he forgot her for fifty years, and she truly hoped it would finally free him from the pain inside him. After all, fifty years is not an eternity.

Judith, who always enjoyed having the last word, decided that now was the time. The voice inside his head left no doubt that she was about to sum it all up.

"We all live — or lived — in a magnificent world, one that is drawn in a myriad of shapes, colored by an endless palette of hues, mixed by an unseen hand. Is that what we call God? I don't know. Call it anything that pleases you. However, try not to fight a war about what you name it; people have been making that mistake for centuries.

"Many people call it Nature. I call it an endless painting," Judith concluded, and punctuated her final thought with a forceful, "*I loved living.*"

Boaz stood up straight as Judith finished. His tears had stopped. He wiped his face and especially his eyes lest any mourner walking by see his saddened countenance. But there were no witnesses to the upheaval in his soul.

On this day, the last funeral had taken place almost an hour ago. The casual visitors to a particular loved-one's grave chose not to stay late on this afternoon in the vicinity of Judith's burial plot.

This graveyard contained almost no one, assuming you only counted anyone who could still be moving from one place to another. Who would stop him from laying his head close to the nameplate near the head of the casket well below the ground? No one would. So he did. And very quickly, Boaz fell asleep.

He dreamed. All the hate he encountered in Buffalo upon his return from a love-filled journey to Hollywood flashed through his dream. This time, however, it did not fill up his being. It flashed its dark aura and then vanished in his dream, replaced by the long and steady years that it took to establish and grow his life in San Francisco.

And then, his dream flashed onward, and he felt the full impact and the utter loneliness of a life without Judith. Boaz had brought her back to life, at least in his own mind, and that gave him great satisfaction. *He had accomplished his goal.*

His dream was briefly interrupted by this thought: what might have happened if he had reconnected with Judith during the time he had sought to call her. Would he have lived his life in Atlanta, or she in Buffalo? Or would they have searched for a place on Earth that they would have called their own?

Boaz struggled to find an answer, just as he remembered initially toying with the same idea in the weeks following their meeting in Hollywood. Boaz had enjoyed that thought years ago, when the possibility existed that it might happen.

However, much too much time had passed. It proved to be too complicated and confusing, too unanswerable, and ultimately, gave him too much hurt to think about where they might have carved their spot on this Earth at this late stage of his life. He put it out of his dream as quickly as it had entered it.

Boaz stirred. What had taken long, long years to transpire passed through his dream in the space of a few minutes. That did not make it less painful to relive, but the harsh effect he endured for all those years had finally vanished, also.

Boaz felt no need to open his eyes. The kaleidoscope of his life had completed its latest turn, and the endless mishmash of his bad decisions left him at last. He felt cleansed. Boaz relaxed into a deep, satisfying sleep.

PHOTO CREDIT. Guy Bianco via

Beautiful Free Images & Pictures | Unsplash

Chapter Nine

Soulmates: Atlanta, 2019

From her hidden perch within the branches of the nearby trees, Scarlett, the falcon who actually ruled this graveyard, became aware of the chill in the late afternoon air. It had become her time to hunt, and she took to the air. With a practiced eye, she scoured the nearby landscape as she flew in slow circles. It did not take long to spot the small pigeon walking unafraid on the ground near Judith's grave as it closed in on the face of a very exhausted Boaz. What that young pigeon might have done to the face of the sleeping giant in front of him, we shall never know.

In less time than it takes to tell about it, the hunter became the hunted. As the bird tried to fly away, the falcon attacked with deadly accuracy the next meal she would bring back to the nest.

Even this magnificent bird could not prevent her feathers brushing Boaz' cheek several times rapidly as she flew, oh, so close. Scarlett's instincts made catching dinner in her talons paramount in her mind. Like her partner-for-life, Rhett, she just did not give a damn about anything else. The pigeon did not have a say in the matter.

Boaz awoke startled and confused. He sat up. Seeing the falcon so close, he thought it was attacking him. He would have been more upset if he had noticed the pigeon. But the sight of a bird of prey this near did not need any amplification in his mind. Unable to understand what was happening, he suddenly became absolutely terrified.

His enlarged aortic aneurysm burst, and he began to bleed out internally. High blood pressure had finally betrayed him. He fell on his back across the gravesite. Judith could gather him in her arms if that were possible. Boaz remained in that slightly awkward position for his last few minutes. He stared at the now cloudy sky with its subdued, late afternoon sun. He thought of that small filing cabinet. Then life passed out of his physical body as his soul went in search of a different soul.

Some twenty-five minutes would also pass before an elderly groundskeeper would find Boaz. For now, though, it was as quiet as a cemetery . . . which, of course, it is.

"Hi-ya, Boaz."

Without intentionally doing harm to himself, Boaz joined Judith for all eternity. Their souls became intertwined as one.

And so, you must realize by now that true love does endure. It knows no boundaries.

THE END

About the Author

PHOTO CREDIT: Sheila Smith.

Harvey Brown was born in Philadelphia and educated at the University of Pennsylvania. He worked for newspapers and TV stations in NYC, Philadelphia, Buffalo and San Francisco. For 13 years, he was Senior Editor, Technion Publications, bridging the gap between technical subjects and easily-read articles. He currently works in property management.

www.ingramcontent.com/pod-product-compliance
Lightning Source LLC
Chambersburg PA
CBHW040537170726
48295CB00012B/504